THE COWBOY'S
SPECIAL CHRISTMAS

BARBARA MCMAHON

1

Cole Martin parked his pickup truck and climbed out, scanning the sky. Snow was predicted. The wind that blew steadily from the west was biting cold. Dark clouds billowed in the distance. Experience told him he'd better hustle. He settled his cowboy hat more securely and headed into the Shop and Save.

The grocery store was practically empty. Most people had done their shopping for Thanksgiving long before now. For a while he'd planned to just make do. But since he was in town today anyway, he decided to check out the frozen dinners to see if there were any with turkey and gravy.

Ordinarily he'd be sitting down tomorrow to the feast his mom made every year. Or as he had last year, spend the day with Gloria and her family.

He shied away from that thought. They were never going to share Thanksgiving again, thanks to her betrayal.

Even the cowboys who worked on the Circle M Ranch had other plans this year.

He was alone–at Thanksgiving–one of the most family-oriented holidays there was.

He headed to the back of the store where the freezer section was. Scanning the boxes, he moved gradually down the aisle toward the only other person looking at frozen foods.

He noted she was staring at the boxes in front of her. Tall, slender and bundled up in a thick coat with a knit cap covering most of her blonde hair. She looked familiar, but he couldn't place her. Was she a cousin of one of the ushers at church? Some friend of Gloria's?

He stepped closer. She was staring at frozen dinners.

She glanced at him, then back at the display.

He stopped next to her.

She looked again. "Am I in your way?" she asked. Her voice was soft.

"No. I'm looking for something for tomorrow." He kept his gaze on the array of dinners-- chicken pot pies; chicken dinners; beef stew; Chinese. Cole frowned. Shouldn't there be turkey dinners with all the trimmings for folks like him?

She held out a slip of paper. "I have a two-for-one coupon. If we choose the same brand, we can share."

He nodded, "Thanks. I'm hoping for turkey with gravy."

She opened the door and reached in near the bottom and withdrew two dinners. "Like these?" she asked, showing him the picture of turkey, dressing, sweet potatoes and what looked like apple crumble in a portion of the tray.

"I guess." He wondered if he should explain that he normally didn't eat frozen dinners for Thanksgiving, but then he thought he didn't need to. She was in the same boat.

"It's the largest they have. Though I'll miss leftovers. I didn't want to do all that cooking for one, but leftovers are my favorite part of Thanksgiving," she said looking at the colorful cover.

"Turkey sandwiches piled high with meat and cranberry sauce," he said. His mother always cooked the biggest turkey that would fit in the oven so they had plenty of leftovers.

She smiled at him. Her eyes sparkled. They were a silvery grey and caught Cole unaware. He could hardly look away.

"I've never had sandwiches with cranberry sauce, but it does sound good."

"The best." He reached out and took one of the frozen dinners, looking at the cover. The photograph made it look wonderful. He knew it would never compare to a home-cooked meal, but he wasn't going to cook either.

"Did you need anything else?" she asked.

"Nope."

"I'm picking up some sparkling cider to celebrate, then I'll be ready to check out and we can share that coupon."

"What are you celebrating?" he asked as they started up the aisle toward the front of the store.

"Thanksgiving, of course. And all the good things that have happened in the last year."

"Oh. Yeah, that sounds right." His mom always made a big deal of going around the table and having everyone tell some of their best memories of the previous year.

He wondered what he had to celebrate this year. He was alone at Thanksgiving. He and the woman he'd been half way in love with had split. He'd finished the house he lived in about a half mile from his folks', but it was scarcely furnished. He'd lost interest when he and Gloria stopped seeing each other.

He was solely in charge of the ranch while his parents cruised down the Amazon. And the approaching storm promised to be a doozy, which meant making sure the cattle had feed and access to water.

She glanced at him again when she paused by the sparkling cider. "Shall we take advantage of this special as well?"

He looked. The cider was marked two for one.

Suddenly he decided he'd like some sparkling cider for dinner. To make it more festive.

"Sure."

Four items on the belt at the checkout stand. She produced her coupon, and the checker rang up the total.

Cole brought out his wallet and handed the clerk a twenty-dollar bill just as she did the same. The checker looked confused.

"We're splitting it down the middle," Cole explained.

"Oh." The young man frowned, but made change for both bills and handed the money to them. "Shall I bag them in one or two bags?" he asked.

"Two," she said.

As they left the store together, Cole paused for a second. "I don't even know your name and we're practically sharing Thanksgiving dinner together."

She smiled brightly and nodded. "Practically. I'm Jennifer Carleton. I'm sort of new in town. This is my first holiday here."

"Cole Martin. From the Circle M ranch outside of town."

"I know that ranch. I treated one of your horses when he was cut badly with barbed wire."

"You're the new vet in town? Dad told me he'd called you in when Smoky's leg wouldn't stop bleeding."

"A few stitches and he was good as new," she confirmed.

Cole nodded, wondering how such a pretty woman had decided to become a large animal vet. It seemed more the job for some robust cowboy used to wrestling with cattle and horses and other ranch stock.

"Well, good night. Happy Thanksgiving," she said, turning to walk to a truck nearby.

"Wait," Cole said.

She turned with an inquiring look on her face.

"We should eat Thanksgiving together. I mean, we bought the food together, why not? I don't have any other plans and it looks as if you don't either. You can come out to the ranch and we'll heat the dinners, drink the cider and spend an afternoon watching the football games."

"Your folks don't have other plans?" she asked.

He held up his bag. "Do you think I'd be eating this if my mother was around? They're on a cruise down the Amazon. I'm alone for the day."

He glanced at the sky again. The storm front looked even closer. Maybe it was a bad idea. If it snowed as much as predicted, he'd have his work cut out for him tomorrow. And he shouldn't ask her to drive out to the ranch in case the roads were bad. "Never mind, bad idea. If it does snow, sometimes the roads become treacherous."

She nodded. "Okay, then, how about you come in to town if the roads are passable. My place is small, but you'd be welcome. Say around one o'clock?"

"Sounds like a plan. Unless the storm changes things. If it does, I'll call you."

She nodded and turned to continue to her truck.

Cole watched a moment, then feeling the icy cold wind, he hurried to his own pickup. For a moment he felt elated. He wouldn't be alone for the holiday after all.

2

Jennifer drove to the small apartment building where she now lived. The apartment was on the ground floor and had a small patio off the dining area. The kitchen was galley style and suited her. She ate a lot of meals at the diner in town or on the fly as she drove to the outlying ranches and farms that needed her services.

She put away her frozen dinner and refrigerated the cider. Her invitation had been impulsive, but she didn't regret it. Since she couldn't be with family this holiday, she was glad she'd spend a portion of it with someone. She was lonely since moving to Wyoming. She had begun attending the local church and had met a few people. She knew some of the ranchers and their wives and knew in time she'd become part of the community. But she didn't know anyone well enough to be invited to Thanksgiving dinner.

And returning home wasn't an option. Not so soon, maybe in a year or two when she could forget the past and the future she'd once thought she'd enjoy.

Refusing to dwell on things she couldn't change, she set about cleaning the apartment from top to bottom in anticipation of her first guest.

It didn't take long. While she vacuumed she thought about Cole Martin. She'd met his father when she'd stitched up that horse. He'd been friendly and talked with her the entire time she was there. Cole resembled him a bit. Both were tall with dark hair. Cole's blue eyes had to come from his mother, she suspected. His father's eyes had been more hazel.

Wyoming was totally different from her home in Texas, but cowboys and ranchers and stock animals were pretty much the same. She loved working with the larger animals and knew she'd found the perfect spot when she had bought out the old veterinarian's practice. Ben Hazlet had introduced her around before moving to Florida to fulfill a life-long dream to live by the sea.

The major difference was the weather. The area near San Antonio didn't have the extremes she knew she could expect here—hot in summer, freezing cold in winter. And the wind was an aspect she'd never anticipated. It seemed to blow all the time.

Still, she was satisfied with her decision to move. It'd be best for all concerned as the years rolled on. Though it was hard this first Thanksgiving away from her family. At some point she'd have to spend a holiday with everyone, but not yet. Not this soon.

Cole woke at four in the morning, rolling out of bed and feeling the cold floor beneath his feet. He dressed quickly. He wanted to see any damage caused by the storm and make sure the animals had access to food and water. And with any luck, he'd be able to get to town by one.

It was pitch black outside as he stood by his sink sipping hot coffee, a bagel with cream cheese in one hand. As far as he could tell from staring into the darkness, the snow had stopped.

Stepping outside only moments later, he was hit full force by the wind. It felt like it came straight from Alaska.

On the other hand, it had kept the snow from piling up. There was barely four inches crunching underfoot as he headed for the barn. He'd feed the horses and make sure they were set for the day. He wouldn't stay late in town and have to repeat the chore again later. There wasn't much to do to feed them and the task was quickly finished.

When dawn began to lighten the eastern sky, he saddled up and headed for the creek that traversed the pasture where they'd driven the majority of the herd last week. There was plenty of grazing for the animals if they could forage beneath the snow. And the creek rarely froze. He had to make sure it hadn't today. Then he'd check the outlying regions for the cattle that hadn't been moved.

It was late morning when he returned to the house. A quick shower, shave, and clean change of clothes and he was ready to go.

As he drove into town, he couldn't help thinking of last Thanksgiving. How much things had changed in only one year. Who knew what the future would hold. He hoped his folks didn't plan on a Thanksgiving trip each year. It sucked to be alone. Not that he resented their trip. It had been a long-held dream for both of them, and he was glad they were able to go this year.

Jennifer wished she had a fireplace in her apartment. She loved her parents' place with the large fireplace in the family room that always had a roaring fire whenever the weather was cold enough. And often they'd have a cold snap around Thanksgiving so everyone watched TV warmly ensconced together celebrating the holiday.

Where they'd all be today except for her.

Trying to ignore the sadness that swept through, she tried to keep busy until her guest arrived. She hoped there'd be no emergencies requiring her services today. If there were, of course she'd respond, despite the weather and her expected guest. He'd understand, she knew. He was a rancher and they all seemed to put their animals ahead of themselves.

She wished now she'd picked up a frozen pumpkin pie for later. The invitation had been spontaneous after they left the store and she never thought of pie until she was home. Oh well, they both had the same meal, it would have to do.

As one o'clock approached she felt vaguely nervous. What if he didn't show up? She looked out the window for the hundredth time. The snow wasn't deep. The wind saw to that. So driving might be okay. Would the ranch have fared well so he wasn't needed to feed cattle or break ice in watering troughs?

The phone rang. Jennifer's heart sank. He was calling to say he couldn't come. She went to the phone on her small desk. It was the extension to her office line. She hadn't given Cole her cell number so if he needed to reach her it would be the office line.

Unless it was someone in need.

"Dr. Carleton," she answered.

"Oh, honey, that sounds so formal. Happy Thanksgiving," her mother said.

"Hi mom. Why are you calling this line? It's my work phone."

"Your cell went right to voice mail. Did the battery die or were you on the phone with someone else?"

Jennifer thought about it for a second. "It needs to be charged, I bet. I'm glad you called. Happy Thanksgiving."

"It's not the same without you here, honey," her mother said softly.

Jennifer didn't respond. Things were as they were.

"Anyway, do you have plans for today?" her mother asked brightly.

"I do. I have a guest coming over so we can eat dinner together." No reason telling her mother they were eating frozen dinners. She'd be horrified.

"Oh, what fun. I was worried you'd end up spending the day by yourself. Who is she? Did you two meet at church?"

"She who?" Jennifer asked.

"Your guest."

"It's a he, Mom. Cole Martin. He's a rancher. I stitched up one of his horses a couple of weeks ago."

Jennifer could hear the commotion in the background. She was one of five sisters—two of whom were married with children. She smiled when she heard the baby cry. Blinking back tears, she knew the next time she saw little Jason he'd have grown so much she might not recognize him.

"Well, that's interesting," her mother said at last.

"No big deal. He's alone today and I am too, so we decided to share dinner. Maybe watch a football game. We hardly know each other. I mean, we just met and all. But he's the son of a rancher I do know and he's nice, too, so I expect like father like son." She closed her mouth abruptly. She was babbling. A tendency when she was nervous. Which she was not.

Not about Cole. They'd truly just met. This wasn't a date or anything.

"Well, you'll have to let me know how the day goes. Here's Susannah to say hi. Then your dad's next in line."

Jennifer didn't ask about Catherine. She hoped her mother was sensitive enough not to put her on the phone.

"Hey, what's interesting? I heard mom say that," Susannah said.

"Not much. How is Jason? I heard him a moment ago."

"He's growing like a weed. We can Skype this weekend and you can see for yourself. We're staying here until Sunday. Miss you, sis. It isn't the same."

"Yeah, well..." What was there to say.

"Have a happy day. Here's dad."

"Hello baby, how are you?"

Her dad's deep voice had her longing more than ever to be in the midst of the family.

"I'm doing well, Daddy. No one seems to object that the new vet is female. I've done some routine work and some emergency calls. Dr. Hazlet was great about taking me as many places as he could to introduce me around before he left. And I found a church I like a lot."

"That's always important. Don't get too tied up in that community you can't take time to get home for visits. Christmas isn't too far away you know."

"I know." She'd have to decide what she would do about that holiday as well. Sighing softly, she wished life could go back to the way it was a year ago.

"They're televising the Texas game, I'm assuming you'll be rooting for the home team."

"Of course. I may be out of Texas but you can't take Texas out of me!"

He laughed. "I miss you, sugar. You take care. Here's Maggie."

Jennifer spoke with another sister, then her oldest niece. When the call ended, she felt a mixture of sadness to be away from home and relieved no one spoke about Catherine or put her on the phone.

3

A knock sounded at her door.

Glancing at the clock, she saw it was already one.

She opened it to see Cole Martin standing there, a plastic bag in one hand, the sparkling cider in the other.

"I come bearing gifts," he said with a smile.

How had she not noticed that dimple last night? His smile was infectious and she smiled back.

"Come in. Is it the cider?" she asked.

"Actually, my folks called this morning and when I told them I wasn't spending Thanksgiving alone, my mom told me about some frozen pumpkin pies she'd made before she left. So I brought one. We need to cook it, but I figure about half time we'd want a snack."

"Perfect. I was wishing I'd thought to buy one last night," she said.

Jennifer watched as Cole took stock of her

small apartment as he shrugged out of his heavy jacket. She took the pie and cider into the small kitchen glad it was open to the rest of the apartment so she didn't feel she was abandoning her guest.

"Can I do anything to help?" he asked, following her.

She handed him the cider. "Do you want some now?"

"We have two bottles if I remember. Let's have some now and the rest with dinner."

She got two goblets from the cupboard and put them on the counter. "If you'll do the honors," she said, opening a drawer and handing him the bottle opener.

"I've heated the oven, so we can pop our dinners in now to heat and when they're done, we'll be all set. I'll bake the pumpkin pie while we eat," she said, withdrawing her frozen dinner from the fridge.

"Sounds like a plan."

He opened the sparkling cider with a pop and poured some into their goblets. Handing her one, he raised the other.

"To not spending Thanksgiving alone."

She smiled and clinked her glass against his. They both took a sip.

"So tell me about life on a ranch," she said. "I'd think there'd be tons of people around so you wouldn't be eating alone."

"We have a half dozen hands, but they all have the holiday off and most are traveling to visit family. Normally my folks are home and open the house to whoever's around, but with them gone this year, the men who usually spend the day with us decided to take off."

"Can you run the entire ranch by yourself?" she asked leaning against the counter. She took another sip of the cold beverage.

"For a couple of days. Mainly now I need to check that the creek's running free and the cattle can graze. The snow didn't pile up so they're fine. I feed the livestock and check to make sure everyone's okay." He shrugged. "Not that much to do that I can't manage for a couple of days. Did you grow up on a ranch?"

"No, my dad's a pharmacist. He owns a drugstore in San Antonio. I grew up in town. I did have access to horses to ride with friends who did live on ranches in the area. And I visited every chance I could get. But I've never actually lived on a ranch."

"How did you get interested in being a large animal vet?" Cole asked, leaning against the counter as she took the frozen dinners out of the cartons and placed them on a cookie sheet.

She smiled. "I get that question a lot. Is it because I'm a woman?"

"Probably. I'm curious, that's all."

"Mostly I think people expect me to be treating fou-fou dogs and fluffy cats. I like larger animals. I find their needs fascinating and for the most part do quite well. Sometimes I need help if I need to reposition a horse or cow, but otherwise I'm fine."

"Are there no openings for vets in San Antonio?" he asked.

She hesitated a moment, taking another sip of cider to stall for time. She didn't know this man and wasn't going to share personal information he really didn't need to know.

"I worked for another vet, but wanted my own practice. When the opportunity came up to buy Dr. Hazlet's practice, I jumped at it."

Anything to get away from San Antonio as quickly as possible.

"Nice to have your own practice at such a young age."

She laughed. "Are you fishing for my age?"

"Nope, I figure you're still on the sunny side of thirty, so you've done a lot at such a young age."

"Well, you're right, I won't be thirty for two more years. And so far I don't regret a single thing about buying this practice. The more I get to know my neighbors, the better things will be." No need to confess she used the money she had been saving for her wedding. The wedding that would never be. It had been enough for a down payment and Dr. Hazlet was generous with payment terms.

"How long have you been in town?" he asked.

"Since July."

"Why haven't I seen you around?" he asked, almost to himself.

"Well, you work on a ranch, I travel around to different ranches. I told you I met your father."

He nodded. "Ever attend Sardis church?"

"Every Sunday I can," she replied.

He looked pensive for a moment. "I don't remember seeing you there."

"It's a fairly good size church. I usually sit midway down on the left side."

"That explains it, we always sit near the front on the right. My folks started sitting there when my brothers and sister and I were little, so we'd be close enough to pay attention to the preacher. Now as much as anything it's habit."

Jennifer put the dinners in the oven.

"It won't be too long, we can sit in the living room until the timer sounds," she said, leading the way. When they were both seated, she on the small sofa and he in her recliner, she smiled. "So you have brothers and a sister?"

"Two brothers, one sister."

"They aren't around, either, for Thanksgiving?"

"My sister married and lives in California. She invited me this year, but it's too far to go for a day. And with no one else to mind the ranch with my folks traveling, that's all I'd be able to spare. One brother's a Marine stationed in Afghanistan. The other's a rodeo cowboy on the circuit down in your neck of the woods. I think he's riding Saturday in San Antonio. How about you? Any siblings?"

"Four sisters."

"Scattered or all still in San Antonio?"

"All in San Antonio. Two are married. No, three now." How could she forget Catherine?

The oven timer sounded and Jennifer went to check on their dinners. Pulling them from the oven, she set them on trivets on the counter.

"I thought we could put everything on china plates to make it more of a holiday meal," she called taking down the dishes from the cupboard near the sink.

They sat at the small dining table near a window that overlooked the small patio and the street beyond. The day remained gray, snow swirling and moving in the wind.

Jennifer had decorated the table for Thanksgiving and she was pleased she wasn't spending the day alone.

During dinner they discussed books they'd read, favorite television shows, and holiday memories from when they were kids.

She enjoyed hearing his stories–they were so different from hers. Not that he monopolized the conversation. He had her match story for story and soon both were laughing at their younger selves and the antics they'd gotten into.

Dinner was finished when the oven timer rang again signaling the pumpkin pie was done.

"I'll get it out and we can let it cool before eating," she said jumping up.

"Mid afternoon sounds right," he said, gathering their dishes and following her into the kitchen. He put them in the sink and ran water over them.

"Leave them, I'll wash them later," she said, carefully placing the steaming pie on a trivet.

"It won't take much time to clean up now if you want. It's not like our kitchen on Thanksgiving. I swear Mom uses every pot and pan in the house and then has her kids do the clean up."

"Then I'll wash and you can dry."

In a short time the kitchen was spotless.

"It makes a difference when there're no leftovers," Jennifer said wistfully.

"Yeah. I'm going to miss turkey sandwiches."

She nodded. They went back to the small living room and she turned on the television. "The game already started, but I'm sure we'll catch up fast," she said sitting beside him.

"And we're watching what?" he asked.

"Texas Aggies of course," she said with a grin.

"Okay, if that's the team to root for. I'm an Aggies fan from way back."

"You went to A&M?" she asked in astonishment.

"Naw, I went to UC Davis, Cal Aggies, for my degree in animal husbandry. I wanted to see some of the world beyond Wyoming."

"Well as one Aggies fan to another, let's hope we win!"

The game was in full progress with only a short time until half-time. The score was tied at seven each. Both Cole and Jennifer were vocal in their approval and disapproval of plays, laughing when they both came to their feet as a long pass and another touchdown resulted.

Jennifer's phone rang.

"Keep watching, I'll take it really quick. It's my office phone, so I might be needed."

She hurried to the kitchen and picked up the phone hoping it wasn't an emergency she'd have to respond to. So far the day had gone great and she didn't want it to end.

"You moved on fast, but still have everyone feeling sorry for you," a familiar angry voice said when she answered.

"Catherine?"

4

"You already have another man on the line. While Joe and I are being treated like pariahs here. The family misses you. Oh how sad you're so far away and couldn't make Thanksgiving at home. You're ruining everything!"

"I'm not the one at fault here, Catherine." Jennifer turned her back toward Cole, knowing she should just hang up and ignore her sister. But she couldn't.

Her sister continued her tirade without stopping. "The kids keep saying they miss Auntie Jennifer and when can they see you again. You're such a drama queen. Get over yourself. Joe chose me. Me! Too bad, so sad for you, but you're ruining what I wanted to be a special first Thanksgiving together. We're pregnant and I wanted everyone to celebrate, but oh, no, they're too sad missing you."

Jennifer quietly hung up the phone, her eyes

stinging. She wanted to be home, but she couldn't bear being around Catherine and Joe. The hurt was too fresh. If they'd stayed away she'd be in the midst of family right now. But she had made sure everyone knew they planned to spend their first Thanksgiving at home.

Now they were going to have a baby. She wanted to cry.

"Is everything okay?" Cole asked. He stood near the kitchen entrance, his voice concerned.

She nodded. "Just give me a minute." She brushed the tears away from her lashes. She needed to get over this. She thought she *was* over it. But her sister's call brought back all the disbelief, the anguish. The heartbreak, the feeling of betrayal by her own sister! Trying to make the best of things, even attending the wedding that had taken a monumental amount of effort.

She'd had to escape Texas, escape the possibilities of running into Catherine or Joe wherever she was in San Antonio. She left behind the home she loved, her friends who kept commiserating with her, everyone dear to her to gain some freedom. Now this!

Couldn't Catherine leave well enough alone?

The phone rang again. She ignored it. She did have an answering service, let them take the call.

"Should I leave? Do you have to go out?" Cole asked.

"No. Don't leave. We haven't had pumpkin pie yet."

The silence stretched out for a long moment.

"What's wrong?" he asked.

All the pent up emotions over the last year burst forth as she turned to face him.

"My sister married the man I thought I was going to marry and now she's blaming me for making their Thanksgiving less fun than others. At least she's home with our mom and dad, my other sisters, nieces and nephews while I'm practically alone a thousand miles away." She felt angry enough to spit nails!

Cole didn't know what to say. He didn't know Jennifer very well, but her outburst hit home. He knew how she felt. Didn't Gloria's betrayal hurt more than he'd ever expected? Hadn't he gone through a dark time not wanting to deal with other people? Wanting no reminders of Gloria and the time they'd spent together? Hard to sidestep when they both lived here.

"Sorry about that," he said inadequately.

The phone rang again. Jennifer looked at it. "What are the chances there's an emergency somewhere?" she murmured.

"Do you need to answer?

"Nope, I have Betty Smythe as my answering service." she said. "She'll try my cell if it's an emergency. Which reminds me, I need to get it charged. Be right back."

She dashed into her bedroom, found her phone on the night stand and quickly plugged it in to charge. A quick glance in the mirror reassured her none of the turmoil she felt roiling inside showed on her face. Taking a deep breath, she vowed to enjoy this day. She wasn't going to let her sister spoil it for her.

She walked into the living room. He was standing near the window, gazing outside.

"Some Thanksgiving, huh. Sorry about that. What can you do about family?" she said.

"Hey, you're entitled. I know some of what you're probably feeling. I broke up with my girlfriend last spring. It takes time to get over a close relationship."

"And are you over her now?" she asked.

He shrugged. "Yeah, I guess. Pretty much. She hooked up with another guy and that was the end of us when I found out. We'd never talked marriage, but we were supposed to be exclusive. If you can't trust someone in a relationship–you don't have a relationship."

"I guess. I never expected my sister to steal him away from me, though," she said sadly.

"He wasn't much of a stayer if another woman could lure him away from you," Cole said, with a smile.

Cole thought Jennifer was beautiful. The afternoon had been really enjoyable. He didn't know her well, but still couldn't imagine a guy turning away from the complete package.

"Thanks, that's a sweet thing to say." She took a deep breath. "Want some pie now?"

"Yeah. That sounds good. It's half time, so get the pie and we can watch the rest of the game."

Once the game was over, with Texas winning, Cole headed home. He needed to take care of the animals before they wondered if they'd been forgotten. It was already growing dark and snow still covered the road in patches.

The visit had been unexpected. He couldn't explain the feeling of protection that rose when Jennifer tried to put on a brave front. He hardly knew her. Yet when she'd explained, he'd wanted to do something to take away the sadness that haunted her eyes.

Which was silly. That was something she had to work through herself. Grief, no matter what the cause, had to be handled individually.

He hoped today wasn't the only time they'd spend together. He wondered if she'd go out with him. Just as a friend. Neither was ready to form a new relationship. Both had baggage they hadn't fully dealt with. Still, it'd be nice to go out together--maybe to dinner and a movie. Or the dance at the Grange held every Friday. Did she like to dance, he wondered?

Sunday morning Cole stood at the back of the sanctuary when he entered instead of heading directly to the spot he and his family usually occupied. Scanning the crowd already gathered, he saw Jennifer where she'd said she sat.

Refusing to give into second thoughts, he headed up the aisle on the left to about half way.

"This seat taken?" he asked her when he stopped at the end of the row.

"Cole! Hi. No, sit down. How are you?"

Jennifer's smile was something he'd never get tired of, he decided. Her eyes sparkled silvery again and her blond hair was soft against her shoulders, cascading halfway down her back in shining waves.

"Can't complain," he responded, sitting next to her.

"You're breaking with tradition," she murmured softly for his ears only. "I thought you sat on the other side."

"Hey, gotta shake things up once in a while. I'll try the view from here today."

"I had a good time on Thanksgiving."

"Me, too. We'll have to do something together again sometime," he said casually, reaching for the hymnal.

"I'd like that."

The service centered on the theme of thankfulness in light of the recent holiday. During announcements, the pastor reminded everyone to sign up for the annual live nativity. The committee had already begun work but needed a few more helpers. Other announcements followed and then the service was over.

As they were walking out of the church, Jennifer asked Cole about the live nativity.

He looked at her. "Want to grab a bite to eat at the diner? I can tell you about it over lunch."

"Okay. That sounds like a plan."

The diner was crowded when Cole and Jennifer arrived, but after a short wait, they were shown to a booth.

"Have you ever eaten here?"he asked as they were handed the menus.

"Every chance I get," Jennifer replied. "It's my home away from my home. It's no fun cooking for one. Plus some days I'm just too tired so I call ahead and take it home. How about you?"

"I don't get to town much during meal times. Sometimes when I bring my mom in for shopping, we'll have lunch here. Good food."

She nodded.

Once their orders were given, Jennifer looked at him. "So tell me about the live nativity the pastor announced."

"We put it on every evening the week before Christmas—seven until eight thirty. The vignettes are erected on the outskirts of the church parking lot, so town folks can drive through. We have iPods we hand out to relate the story of the nativity at each stop and then gather them as the cars are exiting the parking lot. There're several different scenes from the angel announcing to Mary, to her visit with Elizabeth, to traveling to Bethlehem, the scene in the stable with the baby Jesus, shepherds and angels and then the wise men. I was baby Jesus when I was a baby."

She smiled. "How fun. Isn't it too cold to be outside for so long, especially for a baby?"

"Freezing cold some years. But we keep the manger shelter warm with heaters so no babies are harmed in the making. We have heaters in the other scenes, too. It does get cold, but we have extra large costumes to cover."

"So what does the committee do?"

"First it locks in volunteers for the different roles. We need wise men, shepherds, an inn keeper, angels, a woman playing Elizabeth, a young Mary and a Mary at the manger, things like that. And if kids want to join in, we find parts for them. Then we have animals in the stable. I have an old donkey who's been a part of the event for the last eleven years. He doesn't mind standing around munching hay. Sam Parsons has a couple of sheep, Jason Morris has a pony. A couple of rancher kids have 4-H cows we can use. We want it to look authentic."

"Oh, I want to do something. Who do I talk to about it?" she asked.

"Jeff Howard's in charge. I can give you his number. I'm part of the animal brigade. I round up the pony, donkey and sheep for the stable. We have a corral in town we use to keep them in during the day and at night after the performance. Sometimes there's a need for rebuilding sets or erecting them. Martha Joyce is in charge of costume making. The choir director records the program if we change something. The church secretary types up the handout we give each driver. We always invite everyone to Christmas services."

"It's been going on a long time if you were baby Jesus once," she said.

"Yeah, I think my mom was in it as an angel when she was a little girl. The whole town turns out to drive through one night or another. Some families visit every night."

"That sounds like so much fun. I want to help. What can I do?" Jennifer said, already thinking of it as another way to fit into the community and make friends.

"Call Jeff. He'll let you know how you can help. No one's ever turned away."

"Is he in the phone book?"

"You don't have a church directory?"

She shook her head.

"I'll call you later and give you his number. Next time you're in church, the directories are on the far left of the communications area—you know where all the fliers are posted and last week's bulletins are available?"

She nodded. "I know where you mean."

"So, do you think you'll be here for Christmas? Or will you head for San Antonio?"

She started to answer when their food arrived. Soon they were eating and Jennifer tried to figure out how to answer the question. She didn't know. Maybe she'd feel better by Christmas.

Or maybe Joe and Catherine would be away for Christmas and leave the way clear for her.

"Christmas?" he asked again.

5

"I'm not sure. I think it would be too awkward to go home. Plus, who could I get to be on call?"

"Time heals," he said.

She looked at him.

"I was pretty shaken when I found out about Gloria. That was last May. For a while I didn't want to be around anyone and didn't want anyone to speak her name. But life is what it is. Things happen. Even when we hate what they do, that changes nothing. I've come to believe that maybe God has a better plan for me. So I'm letting go of the anger, getting over the hurt, and hoping the future will give me something totally unexpected and special," Cole said.

"Nice philosophy if you can believe it," she murmured.

"We weren't talking marriage. You have more reason to feel hurt," he added.

Jennifer shrugged. She took a deep breath,

determined to ignore the past for the time being and enjoy her lunch with Cole. No need to bring her past into lunch. She'd have time to wallow in pity when she returned to her apartment.

The rest of the lunch passed pleasantly. She was glad for the interlude. Sunday was turning out to be a wonderful day.

Jennifer was humming when she reached her apartment. She'd catch up on some reading, maybe plan her Christmas shopping. If she truly wasn't going home for Christmas, she needed to shop early to beat the mail rush and make sure presents arrived in time.

By mid afternoon, she had made her list and even considered shopping today. But feeling lazy, she decided against it. Time for that mystery she'd been reading whenever time permitted. She really wanted to know the ending.

Her cell rang. Checking the number, she saw it was her mother calling.

"Hi, Mom," she said.

"Hi sweetie. How're you doing?" Her mother's familiar voice struck a nerve of homesickness.

"Great. How about you?" She gazed sadly around her small apartment, knowing her mother was probably in the comfortable family room, or maybe in her sewing room if she was taking a quick break.

"We're almost out of left-overs and your dad is talking about firing up the grill for real meat tonight."

Jennifer laughed. Her father was notorious for thinking beef was the only real meat in the world. He only tolerated turkey on the few occasions they had it.

"Sounds like dad."

"We really missed you on Thanksgiving, sweetie. Are you planning on being here for Christmas. I hope you will be. It's not the same without the entire family."

"Probably not, Mom."

She couldn't bring herself to ask about Catherine's plans. She knew her mother suspected her reasons for not coming home, but didn't want to blatantly state them. "I'm the only vet in town and don't have anyone to back me up if I wanted to take off for a few days."

"What did the former veterinarian do? Surely he didn't work all the time and never take a break."

"He had a deal with another vet from another town for emergency backup. I need to see if we can work a similar deal. But I haven't done it yet."

Her mom was silent for a moment, then asked, "And how did Thanksgiving go?"

"I missed y'all," Jennifer said.

"I meant with your guest."

"It was fine."

"Are you seeing him again?"

"I saw him in church earlier today. And we had lunch together."

"Ummm."

"What does that mean?" Jennifer asked.

"Be careful, sweetie. You're getting over a traumatic event. Don't fall for the first man who comes along. That's a rebound and usually doesn't last."

"Mom! I just met him on Wednesday. He was alone on Thanksgiving and so was I so we spent it together. I have no romantic interest in Cole. And he's also getting over a breakup. No romantic interest for either of us."

"I want you to be happy, but you don't need to get involved right away to show Joe anything. You'll find a good man when it's right and end up not caring a fig that Joe and Catherine fell in love."

"Ummm, we'll see." Jennifer still smarted over her sister and her one-time fiancé marrying so soon after they met. She loved her sister, but the hurt went deep. It would be wonderful if her mother's predictions came true. She'd like to spend a holiday at home in the future.

"So are you planning to see this Cole again?"

"No plans. But I'm going to be doing something totally new for me—I'm going to work on a live nativity. The church I'm going to does this every year. I don't know yet what I'll be doing. I need to call the coordinator to volunteer. Doesn't that sound like fun?"

"Yes it does, tell me more about it."

Jennifer shared all Cole had told her—except the part about his involvement. No sense in having her mother think things were different than they were. Cole had eaten a couple of meals with her, that was all. There was no romance on the horizon.

When they finished talking, the phone rang again. This time it was her office line.

"Hello?"

"It's Cole. I have Jeff Howard's phone number for you."

"Oh, let me get something to write on." She took the phone into the kitchen and pulled a pad from a drawer. "Okay, shoot."

He gave her the number. "Today would be a good day to reach him, since he works during the week at an insurance office in town."

"Thanks, Cole. Did you just get home?"

"Naw I got home a while ago. Took a quick ride out to check on the cattle. The snow isn't melting but the temperature is warm enough to keep the water source free of ice. Might not be the case tomorrow, but several of the cowboys are back so it's not all on me anymore."

"Good. I enjoyed lunch."

"Yeah, me, too. Hope there's something right up your alley with the live nativity."

"Me, too. Thanks for calling."

She hung up and wondered if the call had really been short and abrupt or if she was imagining things.

Maybe he talked to someone who warned him about a rebound.

Not that she thought he'd displayed any interest beyond bare friendship.

She had things to do, not think about a cowboy she'd just met a few days ago. She got her cell and dialed the number for the live nativity coordinator.

Cole hung up from talking with Jennifer, wishing he'd thought of something else to talk about beside giving her Jeff's phone number.

He poured himself another cup of coffee. It was cold outside and he'd been in the wind for a couple of hours. Glad of the warmth in the house, he looked around.

He'd returned to his own home today. Time to move on. At one time while it was being built, he'd tried more than once to picture he and Gloria settling down and making a family. Never could see that. She liked parties and shopping and dancing and all sorts of things he really wasn't into. His mom made a great rancher's wife. A helpmate for her husband.

Somehow he never saw Gloria in that role.

Jennifer's face popped up. He shook his head. He definitely wasn't going to go there.

She was coming off a bad break up. He was well over Gloria. He might not trust so easily in the future, but there was no lasting heartache to dwell on. Unlike what he was picking up from Jennifer.

They'd been engaged. A commitment to work together for a marriage and a future together. He didn't know her sister, but he wondered what she had to cause that man to turn from a commitment made, to shatter a heart he'd once loved.

He'd probably never know.

Now he wandered through the almost empty house.

He had a bed, a dresser and a recliner in front of the TV. That was about all. Even his eating was usually done over the sink, or at the card table he set up in the dining area, or he ate at his folk's home with them and the men.

Pretty dismal.

He didn't want to buy into the cliché that a home needed a woman's touch. He was capable of buying furniture and window coverings–though he liked them pretty open to the outdoors. Not that he could see anything at night, but during the day he could see forever from each room in the house.

So why hadn't he?

Was it secretly he wanted to share his home with someone special and wanted the choices to be jointly made? He could get his Mom's help. But he didn't want that.

Funny, he'd never asked for Gloria's ideas either.

He'd like a place that was as welcoming as Jennifer's had been at Thanksgiving. Maybe he should visit again to get some tips.

Yeah, like he wanted to visit to get decorating tips.

6

Jennifer hurried into the church fellowship hall. She didn't want to be late, but the drive from her last appointment had taken longer than she'd anticipated. Tonight was the first meeting of the live nativity committee. Judging by all the cars in the parking lot, there were a lot of people on this committee and she looked like the last to arrive.

Pausing at the door, she looked at the crowd. Dressed in jeans for the most part the men and women present were chatting in small groups. Laughter rang out from time to time. There were rows of folding chairs set up but so far only a few had been taken.

Slipping off her heavy jacket, she pasted on a bright smile and walked into the room.

"Hi, I'm Teresa Milan," a friendly voice said from her left. Jennifer turned and met the smiling woman beside her. Also dressed in jeans and a heavy flannel shirt, she looked about Jennifer's age.

"Hi, I'm Jennifer Carleton. I take it this is the live nativity committee."

Teresa's laughter bubbled up. "Yeah, not quite what you think of when you think of committee, right? I mean it looks like half the church is here. But this is the first meeting. Then we break into subcommittees and the sizes are more manageable. Did you have a specialty?"

"I told Jeff I'm open to anything."

"Come on, then, and let's get a seat near the front. I'm one of the angels. I love the look of wonder on the kids' faces each year, so I keep to that role. The good Lord knows it's a stretch for me."

Jennifer glanced around as she followed Teresa to some seats on the second row. She hadn't seen Cole Martin yet. Was he coming tonight?

Not that it mattered to her. She was here to volunteer, not to see Cole.

Sort of. She hoped he would be here tonight so maybe they'd have a chance to chat.

Moments later a large bell clanged and everyone began moving to seats. A man sat next to Jennifer on the other side from Teresa. "Hi, I'm Ed Barnes. Are you new here?"

Jennifer introduced herself. "I've been coming to this church since July. This is my first time for the live nativity."

"Please to meet you. July, huh. You the new vet?"

She nodded.

"I run the pharmacy in town. If you ever need anything in a pinch, let me know."

"Nice to meet you, Ed. My dad's a pharmacist in San Antonio."

"Good Evening everyone," a man in front of the group spoke into a microphone. The crowd immediately quieted. "Glad you all could make it. Most of you know the drill. How many are here from previous live nativities?" he asked.

Most of the hands went up. He chuckled. "Wrong question, obviously. How many are here for the first time?"

Jennifer raised her hand and glanced around. There were only a few others with their hands up.

"So for the newbies, please stand and let us know who you are. If you have a special interest, we'll match you up. Starting with you, sir," he said, pointing to a man in the back.

It didn't take long for the few newbies to introduce themselves. Jennifer was last and she turned to face the rest of the group, spotting Cole leaning against the back wall. When their eyes met, he gave a half wave. She smiled and sat back down.

So he was here. She hoped they got a chance to speak.

After opening prayer, Jeff got to work. He explained the rehearsal schedule—most of them in the evening so everyone knew what to expect. And if there were any glitches they'd have to handle them in the dark as they'd have to during their live presentations.

He began calling out names and assigning groups. Jennifer listened for hers and when it was called, to no surprise, she was assigned to animals.

"We've set up subcommittee designations at various areas in the hall, so find your group and get started. I'll stop by each group to answer any other questions."

"Nice to meet you Jennifer," Ed said as he stood. "Maybe we could have coffee together sometime."

"I'd like that," she said with a smile.

Teresa waited for her to walk across the large fellowship hall. "Ed's nice. His father started the pharmacy ages ago and now they work together. His wife died about two years ago, really sad, she had breast cancer discovered too late."

"Oh, I'm sorry to hear that. He seems so young to be a widower."

"I know. Sally was sweet. They were a cute couple. Here's my group. Maybe you and I can have coffee sometime."

"I'd really like that," Jennifer said. So far Teresa was the first woman about her age she'd met in town. It would be great to have a new friend.

It was not surprising to Jennifer to find Cole and two other cowboys standing together near the sign that said animals.

"Jennifer, I'd like you to meet Sam Parsons and Jason Morris. This is our new vet, Jennifer Carleton. Jennifer, these are the two men who also provide animals. Sam has sheep and Jason a pony."

"Nice to meet you both," Jennifer said, shaking hands with the two older men.

A teenage girl walked over and smiled at them. "I'm Maizie Jamerson. I have a cow that can be in the stable. Jeff told me to talk to you all about him."

Introductions were made and the group sat around a small table to discuss bringing the animals, how they would be set up for the live nativity and their care during the week.

While Cole had always taken care of the animals in the small corral near the feed barn in town, Jennifer volunteered as one who lived in town to take care of them to save Cole a trip in to town each morning. All of them would be around in the evenings to transport the animals the short distance to the church and take care of feeding.

"In the past, it's worked well to feed them during that hour," Sam said. "That way they don't get the urge to wander off."

"So Jennifer and I can take care of getting the corral ready for the animals. We'll need them there three days before the first night to get them used to it, and for final rehearsals," Cole said.

"I can help, too," Maizie said. "It'll look good on my 4-H project."

"Good, we can use the help," Jennifer said. "Is it only a corral, or is there a shelter, too."

"One side open shelter, area for feed, corral that hasn't been used since last year," Jason said. Might have to check the weeds to make sure there's nothing noxious there."

"How about we meet on Saturday," Cole suggested.

Maizie nodded. "What time?"

He looked at Jennifer.

"I'm game. Say around nine?" she replied.

"Okay, see everyone on Saturday."

As the group rose, Maizie hurried over to another group with teenagers in it.

"Probably would rather be with them than us old fogies," Sam said with a grin.

"I'm surprised there aren't more 4-H kids with cattle," Cole commented.

"Maybe she'll talk another two or three to join in," Jason said. "See you." He ambled over to another group and sat beside an auburn-haired woman.

"I'll walk you to your truck," Cole said to Jennifer as they both headed for the exit door. "I didn't expect you on this group. I thought you'd want a role in the vignettes."

"No, I told Jeff when I talked with him I could handle the animals. And I think it works out that I can feed them in the mornings. Saves the rest of you coming in just to feed them each day."

"I didn't mind, but can't deny it'll be a help. Especially if we get more snow."

"Which we are likely to?" she asked.

"Yeah, another storm or two before Christmas. I hope it's not below zero the nights of the live nativity."

She donned her jacket, already anticipating the cold outside. Soon she'd be in her warm apartment. But on the performance nights, it would mean more than an hour and a half standing in the cold. She hoped for a warming spell.

"Good night," she said when she reached her truck.

"Glad you joined us," Cole said as he continued on to his own truck.

Jennifer got in and started the engine. The air from the vent wasn't as warm as earlier, but still warmer than outside air. She watched as he drove past and waved. She smiled, also glad she'd joined them.

7

Jennifer entered the diner late Friday morning, looking around for Ed Barnes. He'd called last night to invite her to coffee. She'd had two appointments out of town, but called on her way in from the last one. She was a couple of minutes late but had warned Ed she still wasn't good on judging how long it took her to get from place to place.

She saw him in a booth toward the back. When he saw her he waved and stood up.

"Hi, sorry I'm late," she said.

"No problem. I've only been here a couple of minutes." He helped her take off her jacket and put it on the hook on the post between booths.

She slid in one seat and smiled when he slid in opposite her.

"Coffee?" he asked.

"Yes. And maybe a slice of their cinnamon swirl coffee cake," she said.

Ed placed their order and looked at her. "Where did you say you were this morning?"

"Stevens' place. Something got in their hen house and really did a job on killing a number of their hens. There were three badly injured, but I think they might pull through. I hate stuff like that."

"I bet Bob Stevens hates it worse," Ed said dryly.

She nodded. "I'm sure. He's fixing to get a guard dog. He thinks it was a coyote."

"Better that than a mountain lion. No wonder it took you so long to get here after your call, they live more than thirty miles out of town. How far do you go normally?"

"Wherever I'm needed. I'm the closest vet to most of the ranches in the entire county, so I really cover a big area. Thankfully, so far there haven't been any simultaneous emergencies or disasters."

Ed looked over toward the front. "I hope this won't be a potential disaster either," he murmured.

Jennifer leaned over and looked over her shoulder to the front. More people were coming in, but wasn't that the point of the diner?

"What do you mean?" she asked, sitting back and facing Ed.

"Cole Martin is sitting at the counter. Gloria Hopper just walked in."

Jennifer looked at the long counter against the wall. She hadn't even glanced there when she came in. Third cowboy from the end was Cole.

"So his ex," she murmured.

Ed looked surprised. "You know Cole and Gloria?"

"I know he used to date Gloria. And they broke up."

Ed nodded. "Rumor around town is Cole wasn't coming up to scratch in asking her to marry him and she tried to make him jealous. Only it backfired and he dumped her."

"Wow." She looked over her shoulder again immediately knowing who Gloria was. It was the stunning brunette already walking right up to Cole. They were too far away for her to hear anything, but she couldn't stop looking.

It did not look like a harmonious meeting. Gloria put her hand on his shoulder and he shook it off. Turning his back, he continued to sip the cup of coffee he held in his hands.

Jennifer knew she should turn back to Ed, but she was mesmerized. Was Gloria trying to make amends?

Their order arrived and Jennifer reluctantly returned her attention to Ed Barnes. "Sorry, I was just curious," she murmured.

"I don't blame you. Seems like half the people here are watching them. I didn't know you knew Cole."

"We shared Thanksgiving dinner together. And now we're on the live nativity group handling the animals."

Ed nodded, added cream to his coffee and smiled. "How are you settling in?"

Jennifer told him about finding her apartment, the practice, some of the ranchers she'd met. And obviously she attended Sardis Church. She asked him about his business. Time seemed to fly by and when they had finished their coffee and conversation, Jennifer was a bit disappointed to see as she was leaving that Cole had already left.

"We'll have to do this again soon," Ed said as they stood on the sidewalk.

She nodded. "I'd like that. Thanks for today." She smiled as she turned to head back to the small office she rented. Ed was nice. But he wasn't the one she was thinking about as she drove the short distance and parked in front of the building.

She wished she'd seen the result of Cole and Gloria meeting. Had he been willing to listen to whatever Gloria had told him? Was she trying to reconcile? Had she really tried to make a man jealous by hooking up with someone else?

Not her business.

Thankfully as soon as she entered the office the phone rang and she was back to business.

Cole finished his business at the feed store and headed back to the ranch. His folks were coming home tomorrow, so he'd finish up on any tasks and have the next day to pick them up in Cheyenne.

He was still annoyed that Gloria had accosted him in public at the diner. He remembered his manners but his initial inclination had been to walk out on her. She sat on the stool next to him, apologized again for the way they'd ended their relationship and asked for a second chance.

He'd said he'd moved on and didn't want to go back.

That had not set well with her.

Too bad. Once burned, twice shy. And once trust was broken, it was really hard to trust again.

She'd not been happy and told him they were not over.

How she could expect him to start up again with her was beyond him. It'd been months and to his surprise, he felt no tug of interest in her at all when she sat down. Maybe he had moved on and hadn't realized it.

He wanted to tell Jennifer. Let her know that things changed sometimes without being aware of the change until confronted with a situation that ended unexpectedly. He smiled as he drove back to the ranch. He was free of Gloria and ready to move on as he'd told her.

The only hesitation he had was in calling Jennifer. He'd seen her when she'd come into the diner and almost called to her to join him when he saw she was headed directly to Ed Barnes in one of the booths toward the back.

He'd watched for a moment, then tried to ignore them. Nice of Ed to ask her for coffee.

Had he asked for dinner or something else?

He liked Ed. He liked Jennifer. But the two of them together was not something he'd anticipated. He wanted her himself.

Whoa. He almost slammed on the brakes when that thought flashed into his mind.

Granted, she was pretty, interesting, kind and coming off a bad breakup that probably put her off men for life.

Yet they'd shared lunch last Sunday. And when he said they'd have to do it again, she'd agreed. And she'd had coffee with Ed today.

Time to put it to the test.

When Cole reached home, he headed into his house instead of to the barn.

Calling her office line, he hoped she answered and he didn't have to leave a message with Betty Smythe. She'd ask the reason for the call and he'd rather her not know.

"Dr. Carleton," Jennifer said.

Relieved, he relaxed. "Hey, it's Cole. I wondered if you wanted to catch dinner Saturday and maybe drive into Wilcox to see a movie." Their own town was too small to have a movie theater, but the drive to Wilcox took less than an hour.

"Sounds nice. What time should I be ready?"

"About six? It takes a while to get to Wilcox. I'll see what's playing and let you know Saturday morning when we meet at the corral."

"Okay. Let me have your cell number, in case I get called out for an emergency," she said.

He rattled it off and then asked for hers. In the future he could bypass Betty.

When he hung up, there a sappy grin on his face. Stupid—he was acting like a teenager. But it felt good after feeling let down these last few months.

8

Right at nine on Saturday morning the animal team showed up at the corral. The men had brought rakes and shovels and work gloves. Jennifer and Maizie quickly walked through the area.

"This needs a lot of work," Maizie said, looking at the weeds that had flourished all summer. The lean-to barn had remnants of feed from last year, which had by the looks of things been great meals for mice. Peering into the bin at one end, Jennifer noted it was tight and in good shape with no sign of mice dropping in it. That's where they'd have the feed for the animals.

"Which is why we're here today. I'm glad the men brought the shovels and rakes, I didn't even think about it."

"I think Cole stopped by one day this week to assess things," Jason said walking up to them. I brought my wife's gloves, they should fit." He handed a pair to Jennifer and one to Maizie.

Where do we start?" Maizie asked, looking overwhelmed.

"If it's okay with the rest of you, Maizie and I will start in the lean-to," Jennifer said.

"That works for us. We'll start at the far end of the corral and work our way to the lean-to. I'm bringing in my truck so we can load it up with debris," Jason said.

"I can offer mine, too, if we need it," Jennifer said.

"If we need it, I'll let you know."

Jennifer and Maizie began tackling the littered barn. First they began raking all the debris out into the corral area. Then they used the shovels to chop the weeds so they could be raked. Dust flew around and soon both of them were sneezing. And laughing.

"So is this your first time like me?" she asked.

"No, I've been doing this since fourth grade. Our Sunday School teacher back then insisted we all play angels. It was lots of fun, and funny too, when Bobby Silva fell off the stand but had a safety rope on, so he looked like he was flying. Only it was in the back and no one could see him." She laughed at the memory.

"Does Bobby still participate."

"Of course. He's a shepherd this time."

"And you're an angel?"

"No, I get to play the Mary with the Angel Gabriel scene. We pantomime, so we don't have to learn any script. And it's still an important part of the nativity story."

"It is."

"Do you have a part?" Maizie asked.

"No, I'm dealing with the animals. I think that's enough for my first time."

"Yeah, maybe. You'll get to drive around and see everything during the performance. None of the rest of us get to."

"I hadn't thought about that," Jennifer said. She wiped her forehead with the back of her hand and Maizie laughed.

"Now you have dirt on your face," she said.

"Great."

Looking over to where the men were working, Jennifer was surprised to see Gloria coming through the gate.

"Oh," she said involuntarily.

Maizie followed her gaze and stopped working.

"This is like a soap opera my grandma likes to watch," the teen said softly. "Will he take her back or not?"

Jennifer looked at her. "The whole town knows?"

Maizie shrugged, her gaze still on the scene unfolding. "Sure, we're a small town. Most everyone likes the Martin family, all of them. So it's interesting to watch. My mom said that Gloria was a fool to play games."

The two of them watched as Gloria approached Sam first, and when he shook his head, she walked over to Cole. He didn't stop work, chopping down weeds. Gloria talked for a few minutes, then in frustration turned and looked around the corral. Spotting Jennifer and Maizie, she walked over to them.

"I came to help, but there aren't enough tools. Can I borrow a rake or shovel?"

"We're using them," Maizie said quickly.

"You can't use both at the same time," Gloria said. She looked at Jennifer. "We haven't met, I'm Gloria Monroe. Cole's a friend of mine."

"Hi, I'm Jennifer Carlton."

"She's the new vet," Maizie volunteered avidly watching Gloria.

Jennifer tried not to smile, but she suspected Maizie was hoping for something dramatic to happen so she could share it with her Mom. And probably every other teenage girl in town.

"Oh. Anyway, if I had a rake, I could help the guys."

"We can use help here," Maizie said. "See the piles we've made so far, they need to get into the back of one of the pickup trucks so we can take it out of here."

Gloria looked at the piles, a frown on her face.

"It'd be a big help and everyone on the team would appreciate it," Maizie said.

Gloria glanced back at Cole and then nodded. "Okay. Which truck is Cole's?"

"We're using mine for the barn stuff," Jennifer said without thinking.

Gloria looked at her. "Fine. Which one is it?"

"I'll bring it in." Handing her rake to Maizie, she headed for her truck. In only moments she parked it near the make-shift barn and lowered the tailgate.

Maizie's eyes sparkled as she watched Gloria scoop shovels full of weeds, old straw and mice droppings and put it in the truck bed.

Returning to their work, Jennifer could swear the teen worked harder than ever to make sure there were plenty of piles for Gloria.

Finally they were satisfied the place was ready for the animals. The three men had worked hard and reached the barn. Before long all the piles were gone, pickups loaded high.

"Where do we dump this?" Jennifer asked as she shut her tailgate.

"Follow me. We'll use an area out of town that's for land fill and green waste," Cole said.

"I can go with you," Gloria said to Cole. "Help empty the trucks."

"We can manage," he replied tightly.

"Thanks for your help today," Jason said kindly. "Will you be part of the live nativity?"

"I can help with the animals."

"No need," Jennifer said with a bright smile. "I'm taking morning duties and Cole and I will handle the evenings as well."

"Oh." Gloria narrowed her eyes as she stared at Jennifer. "Isn't that just peachy."

"It works out well for me," Cole said with a smile at Jennifer. "Follow me and we'll get this stuff dumped and then we can have lunch together."

"All of us?" Maizie asked, her gaze going between Cole, Jennifer and Gloria.

"All who worked," Sam said. "You ride with Jennifer and we'll meet at the diner as soon as we're done."

"I'll wait for everyone there," Gloria said walking toward the gate.

Cole watched her walk away. He didn't know how to make it any plainer to her that he had no intention or interest in rekindling any relationship between them.

Jason stopped as he walked toward his truck. "She's going to be hard to dump. Especially on a church event."

"I told her we're through, don't know what more I can do."

Jason looked after Gloria a moment and then slapped Cole on the back. "Show her would be the best way. Find someone else and be inseparable until she gets it."

Cole nodded, his thoughts immediately going to Jennifer. He'd like to know her better any way. He wondered if she'd agree to improvising until Gloria stopped trying to turn back the clock. Maybe he'd ask at dinner tonight.

Lunch turned out to be better than Cole expected. Maizie and Jennifer flanked him on either side and Gloria ended up sitting between Jason and Sam—boy-girl all around. Gloria didn't make a scene, but he knew she wasn't pleased with the way the seating turned out.

Penny was their waitress and she wrinkled her nose when she stopped at their table. "Is this the work crew?"

"Corral cleanup," Jason said. "We all washed up before coming in."

"Yeah, well, we can still tell." She grinned. "I love the live nativity and am glad it's that time of year again. What'll you have?"

Gloria tried to corner Cole when lunch was finished, but he rose when Jennifer did and walked out with her.

"I'll be by at six," he said.

"I'll be ready," she said with a smile.

Goodbyes said, Jennifer walked to her truck. Before she opened the door, however, Gloria was there.

"Is there something going on between you and Cole?" she asked bluntly.

9

Jennifer looked at her. "We're friends. I'm new in town and he's been friendly."

"He's taken," Gloria said.

"I doubt it. From what I see, he's a man of integrity and would not be seeing someone else if he was involved with anyone," she said evenly, not wanting to give away that she knew what had happened.

"Well, he is. We are working things out. Find another friend." With that Gloria walked back to the sidewalk and toward her own car.

"That was interesting," Jennifer murmured as she got into her truck. She couldn't wait to take a shower and get all the dust and grime off. And decide what to wear to dinner.

Jennifer stood in front of her closet a few hours later trying to decide what to wear. Cole wouldn't be here for another thirty minutes and she was still dithering on her outfit.

The phone rang.

She scooped up the office phone and answered, "Dr. Carleton."

"Help. Please. Hurry. This is an emergency," a frantic voice said on the phone. "One of my bulls has been attacked by a mountain lion and is in bad shape. Oh hurry. I don't want him to die. I can't lose him. Can you come right away? I don't want to lose him."

Jennifer knew the value of a good bull. She hoped she could save him.

"Who is this?"

"The Bar K Bar ranch. We're out on highway 73 about twenty-five miles out of town. Oh, hurry. You can't miss the gate, please, please!"

Jennifer wasted no time in throwing on her jeans, a warm flannel shirt and pulling on warm wool socks. Stomping into her boots, she was ready. Quickly, she called her answering service and told Betty she would be out on a call and where.

"Oh, dear, Hank sets such store by that bull. I hope you can pull him through, doc."

Shrugging into her warm jacket, she dashed to the door. When she opened it, Cole stood there hand raised.

"Oh," she said.

"I know, I'm a bit early." He looked at her attire. "Too early?"

"I just got an emergency call to help an injured bull. I was going to call you on the ride out to the ranch. I can't go to dinner, I have to help."

"Right, where are you going? I'll go with you."

She looked at him. He wore a sports coat and white shirt opened at the throat. His jeans were new, his boots shiny.

"No, you don't have to go. I need to hurry." She locked her door and hurried out to her truck, he kept pace with her. "Do you know the Bar K Bar ranch?"

"Yes, Hank Bufford's place. He runs some fine cattle."

"His bull's been injured by a mountain lion."

"No! Hank loves that bull, his best traits are strong in his offspring. Of course you have to go. I'll drive."

"No, I'll be fine. I just need to get there as quick as I can."

"I'll drive you."

"Who knows how long I'll be there.'

"Who cares. You were my plans for tonight, so we'll still spend it together, but instead of a nice dinner, we'll be wrist deep in blood and sutures."

"Gosh, that sounds romantic!"

Stupid! This wasn't a romantic dinner. They were new friends going to eat together and catch a movie. How could she have said such a thing?

"My truck's right here," he said as they stepped out of the apartment.

It was already completely dark so Jennifer was glad Cole drove. He knew where the ranch was and wouldn't miss it even in the dark.

"Did Hank say how it happened?" Cole asked as they sped up on the highway. The two lane road was straight as far as she could see, which made it easy to keep speed up. Time was of the essence if she wanted to save that bull.

"It wasn't a man who called, some frantic woman." She looked at the dashboard. He was really pushing the limit on the highway.

"His wife Tabitha, then. Frantic doesn't sound like her, though."

"I guess when you're afraid you'll lose your best bull, seconds count. The call was definitely frantic. How much farther?"

"Are we there yet?" he said with a chuckle.

"What?"

"You sound like a kid asking two seconds after we left if we were there yet."

She took a deep breath and blew it out. "I'm just keyed up. I hope we are in time. I know what a blow losing a good bull is to a rancher." And she fervently hoped she could save the bull. It would go a long way in establishing her credibility with the ranching community.

The night closed around them as they were the only car on the highway. The headlights slashed through the darkness as they sped along. Another glance at the dash and Jennifer noticed he was going faster than the speed limit. She hoped they'd be in time.

"It's odd." Cole said a moment later.

"What is?" Willing them to get there sooner wouldn't change physics. They would get there when they got there.

"Last I heard, Hank keeps the bull in a pasture away from the house, and the cows. He must have been out checking on something to see him. He couldn't see the bull from the house."

"I don't know how they knew. Just that I'm needed," she said. "It's been so cold, I expect he has to check watering holes as well."

"Yeah. I hope you can save it. He's a good bull, not that old, plenty of years ahead if he makes it."

Twenty minutes later Cole turned onto a drive with a high arch overhead claiming the Bar K Bar ranch. Jennifer might have missed it in the dark, so she was doubly glad Cole was driving.

When they pulled into the area by the house, outside lights flickered on.

Getting out of the truck, Jennifer grabbed her bag and hurried toward the door that opened. A tall man stood in the light.

"Howdy, folks. Oh, Cole. It's you. What are you doing out here?"

"I drove the vet. Have you met Jennifer Carleton yet, Hank?" Cole asked as he stepped up on the porch beside Jennifer.

"Haven't had the pleasure. Nice to meet you."

"You, too. Where's the bull?" She was anxious to get to her patient. Minutes could make the difference.

"My bull? What do you want with my bull?" he asked looked perplexed.

"To help, if I can."

Hank looked at Cole. "I don't know what she means."

"Was your bull injured by a mountain lion?"

"Not old Barney. That critter's meaner than a junkyard dog. I'd like to see a mountain lion even get in a scratch. Where'd you hear that?"

"I got a call for help," Jennifer said. "The caller clearly said the Bar K Bar. There isn't another ranch around with a similar name that I could have gotten mixed up, is there?"

"Nope, I'm the only one with Bar K Bar, don't know of any other using anything close to that brand. I didn't call."

"How about Tabitha?" Cole asked.

Hank shook his head. "You two come on in. It's cold out here."

Stepping inside, he waited until Cole and Jennifer were inside and closed the door.

"Tabitha, did you call for a vet?"

An older woman came down the hall, wiping her hands on a dish towel. "Why would I call a vet?" She smiled when she saw Cole.

"Hey, Cole. How are you?"

"Doing fine. Tabitha, this is Jennifer Carleton, the new vet in town. She got a call from here saying your bull had been attacked by a mountain lion."

Tabitha shook her head slowly. "Wasn't me. I haven't seen that bull in days. It's too cold for me to go out riding these days."

Jennifer began to relax, trying to recall every word from the phone conversation. She was sure the woman had said the Bar K Bar.

"I'm thinking it's a hoax," Cole said slowly.

"Now who would do such a thing? Getting you way out here on a Saturday night? Sorry for your trouble, Doc, but last I saw, old Barney's doing fine," Hank said. "Tabitha and I are just finishing dinner, but you're welcome to sit a spell and share dessert."

"Thanks, Hank. We made other plans. Which we had to postpone for this."

Jennifer heard the anger in Cole's voice. Who would play–Gloria? She'd heard earlier that Cole was picking her up at six. Had she done this to disrupt their evening?

If Cole hadn't arrived early, it would have worked. As it was, if she did such a thing, she had disrupted their plans.

From the tenseness in Cole, she knew he believed the same thing.

"Nice to meet you, both. And I'm glad it's under these circumstances rather than over an injured bull," Jennifer said with a bright smile. She wanted to leave so she could vent!

"We'll take off. See you," Cole said.

"You two drive carefully. Good night."

Cole entered the highway back to town before he spoke. "I think I know what happened."

"Me, too. Your friend Gloria stopped me earlier and told me you two are involved and to back off."

"You're kidding!" Cole glanced at her. "I can't believe it. I don't know what more I can do to make her understand we're done."

Jennifer shrugged. "Maybe things aren't over for her," she said gently.

They drove in silence for a while. Then Cole spoke.

"I didn't expect Gloria at the corral today."

"She's not really part of the team," Jennifer said, not sure why he felt the need to explain that to her. It was pretty obvious he hadn't expected her.

"Jason said something before we left for lunch," he said thoughtfully.

"Oh?"

"He said I need to show Gloria we're done, not just tell her over and over."

"Sometimes actions do speak louder than words. So what did he suggest?"

"I start seeing someone else, make a big deal of it. You know, dates, and sitting together in church, arriving at the rehearsals together, that kind of thing," he said quickly.

Jennifer's heart rate increased. She slowly slid her damp palms across her jeans.

"Did Jason suggest someone?"

"No. That he left up to me." He glanced at her again, trying to judge her expression in the dark. "I know we've just met. And I know you're not looking for a relationship. Neither am I. So it'd be perfect. We'd both know going in it's just make believe."

"You want me to pretend to be your new girlfriend?"

"Yes. What do you say?"

10

"I think you have rocks in your head."

He laughed. "It does sound a bit bazaar, but maybe it would work. She pretty much left me alone after we broke up. But lately she's popping up wherever I am–like I believe in coincidence."

"Maybe she genuinely loves you and wants another chance."

"Well, she's not getting it."

"She wanted you to propose."

"What?" He looked at her. "Where did you hear that?"

"From Maizie. She said the whole town knew Gloria was trying to make you jealous by going out with that other guy."

"Oh great, now the whole town is invested in my private life."

"Small town," she murmured.

Cole frowned and remained silent as the miles sped by.

They reached town before he spoke again. "So will you?"

Jennifer had been thinking about his outlandish idea since he made it. Why not? If it helped him out, she could play a part for a little while. "For how long?"

"I don't know, until Gloria gets tired of trying to get back together I guess. Say until the first of the year? We could reevaluate then. Besides, you'll have an escort to all the Christmas festivities, the dance at the Grange Hall and New Year's celebration."

"Then we break up and I hope the town doesn't blame me," she said.

"I didn't think about that. Would it hurt your practice?"

She shrugged. "Maybe we keep it casual and light and no one will expect forever. Not like that's going to happen," she ended up bitterly.

He reached over and took her hand, closing his around it. "You know, we don't always know God's plan. Maybe he sent you here to help me out."

She wrinkled her nose. "What about his plan for me?"

"You got a practice at a young age, isn't that enough for now?"

"I guess. And I'm participating in my first live nativity which is really cool."

"So you'll help me?"

"Sure, cowboy, why not? But only if you guarantee me your ex-girlfriend isn't going to sabotage other aspects of my life. If you hadn't arrived early, I'd have already been gone and we wouldn't have the evening together."

"But we do. It's too late to go to Wilcox, but how about the diner in town?"

"My favorite place," she said with a smile, relishing the feel of his hand holding hers. She and Cole were becoming friends. Now to find a few other friends in town to make her feel more a part of the community.

The diner was half empty when they arrived. Both ordered hamburgers with the works and French fries. While they waited Jennifer asked him about Christmas activities in town.

"This town goes all out at Christmas. You've seen the decorations already going up on Main Street. Then there'll be a Christmas Parade the Saturday before Christmas ending up at the square where we light the big tree. Santa will be holding court at the courthouse, and all the kids who visit get candy canes and assurances they'll have a happy Christmas. That all happens right around dark, so folks end up coming for a look at the live nativity afterward."

"Does Santa arrive on a sleigh?"

"Only if we have snow. Otherwise, he just walks down the stairs from the double doors at the court house. Then there's the Christmas dance at the Grange Hall. Everyone goes, old and young. Some dance, others visit with friends and kids run around. It'll start before we wind up the live nativity for the night, but goes on until midnight so we have time to go. Is San Antonio too cosmopolitan to hold such events?"

"There're lots of things going on. But San Antonio's too big to get everyone in the city involved in one project."

"Not always a bad thing. You have some anonymity in a city."

She grinned at him. "You're thinking about the whole town knowing about you and Gloria," she guessed.

"Yep. And us." He reached across the table and took her hand again, gently rubbing his thumb on the back.

She felt a frisson of excitement. "For show, right?" she asked.

He nodded, gazing into her eyes.

"Here you two go," the waitress said setting down the large plates piled high with a burger, toppings and fries. "Need anything else?" she asked, looking from Cole to Jennifer.

"Looks good," Cole said.

As they ate, Cole asked her about her family's Christmas traditions.

Jennifer grew homesick as she told some of the activities her family did at Christmas, from opening one present on Christmas Eve, to midnight services at their church, to the beignets her mom always fixed for Christmas morning.

She'd miss all that this year.

"Beignets? Those French thingies with tons of powdered sugar?"

"Yes, French donuts. Best treat in the world," she said.

"Can you make them?"

She nodded, "But they're never as good as my mom's. Almost, though."

"So we could invite you to the ranch on Christmas Eve and you could fix them for all of us early Christmas morning?"

She looked at him warily. "I suppose I could."

"I'll talk to my mom. She and dad are home from their trip. I bet she'd love to have beignets for breakfast on Christmas."

Cole knew his mother would be happy to meet Jennifer. She'd been worried about him since last spring. Of course, he'd have to make sure she didn't start seeing anything that wasn't there—no false hopes or expectations.

He drove Jennifer home and got his own truck for the drive out to the ranch. For the first time in a long while he felt motivated to fix up his house a bit.

He was up early the next morning and headed for his folks house. His mother would have a pot of coffee on the stove. He'd eat with them, then drive into town with them for church.

And he'd better let her know why he wouldn't be sitting with them today.

"I look forward to meeting her," his mother said when he explained the situation. "She sounds nice if she's willing to help out after so recently meeting you."

"Yeah, well she had a similar situation so I guess we sort of understand where each other is coming from. I figure by New Year's Gloria will have gotten the message."

"Ummm," his mother said. "I suspect she'll get the message but will she heed it? That's one tenacious young woman. Tell me more about Jennifer."

"I've met her. A competent young woman," Cole's father said.

Cole tried to explain the situation—which he hoped would end Gloria's pursuit without a huge dramatic confrontation. Both his parents seemed open and interested, and he could tell by the glances they gave each other from time to time they were withholding judgment until they saw more.

"It's just temporary," he reiterated.

"We'll play along," his father said.

"What? No, there's nothing for you two to do."

He hoped his parents didn't think they had to gush over her or something. That'd spook Jennifer and make Gloria suspect something was up. They'd never been more than cordial with Gloria.

"Except invite her to Christmas Eve at the ranch and to stay over and fix breakfast. You did tell her we'll also have the cowboys who don't have elsewhere to go at Christmas, right?" his mom asked.

"I might not have mentioned that," Cole said. "I will." This was starting to sound like a bigger deal than he'd thought it'd be. Maybe he should reconsider things.

11

Cole slipped into the pew Jennifer usually sat in. She hadn't arrived, and he felt a bit awkward sitting by himself so far from his parents. He could feel the curious glances others around him were giving. He hoped Jennifer arrived before Gloria or things could get a bit sticky.

"Good morning," Jennifer said, sitting next to him. "You arrived bright and early."

"Good morning."

She wore wool slacks and a pretty pink sweater; her cheeks were pink and her silvery eyes were bright.

"So we start," she said softly leaning in closely so only he could hear.

"And it's a good start, from what I can tell," he said, glancing around at the people looking their direction.

She nodded and smiled.

"After services, how about lunch at Jose's. It's the best Mexican food around."

"I've tried it a time or two. You're on. I love it."

"You'll have to give me a ride home. I came in with my folks."

"Sure. Unless I get a call, then you'll have to ride along."

The organ began playing and conversation stopped as the church service began.

Cole spotted Gloria across the church looking around. He quickly averted his eyes and vowed not to look that way the rest of the service, though curiosity was rampant to know if she saw him with Jennifer.

Once the service ended, they hurried to her car and took off for Jose's. It was crowded at the restaurant so they took a seat on the long bench in the lobby area with others waiting for a table. Several of those waiting knew Cole and spoke to him. He introduced Jennifer to each one.

Maizie and her family entered. She made a bee line to Jennifer.

"Hi. Mom, come meet Jennifer. She and I cleaned the stable yesterday."

Anna and her husband Mark walked over and introductions were made.

"I love Mexican food," Maizie said. "We come here a lot. Do you?" She looked at Jennifer.

"Occasionally. I like it, too."

Maizie looked at Cole and back at Jennifer and grinned.

Cole studied the teen. She looked like the cat that swallowed the canary. What was going on between the two of them?

"Cole, your table's ready," one of the waiters came to the lobby. "Hi Mr. and Mrs. Jamerson, it'll be a short wait."

"Fine, Josh," Mark Jamerson said.

"Hi Josh," Maizie said to the young waiter. "Bring lots of chips to our table when we get it."

"Will do, Maizie!" He grinned at her and then seemed to remember why he was there and led Cole and Jennifer to their table.

As they walked, other diners called out greetings to Cole.

Once seated, Jennifer leaned closer. "Do you know everyone in town?"

"Seems like it, doesn't it. You've met a fair share today."

"And I'll never remember all their names."

"That'll come. What looks good to you?"

Jennifer wanted to say, you do. Surprised at the thought, she hid behind her large menu. This was make believe. She had a part to play and while she'd never done drama in school, she felt she could rise to the challenge.

At least she hoped she could. She peeped at him over the top of the menu. He was studying his. For a long moment she couldn't look away. He was a rugged handsome man. From what she knew of him, he was the sort of man any woman would like to know better. No wonder Gloria didn't want to let go.

He glanced up and she looked away quickly. She couldn't be mooning over a guy she'd only met a short time ago. Deciding on enchiladas, she closed the menu and placed it carefully on the table before looking up at him again.

"Decided?"

She nodded and told him what she wanted.

While waiting for the food, Cole gave her a brief bio on some of the people she'd met today, starting with Maizie's folks and ending up with the young man who served them.

He invited her to go riding when she took him back to the ranch. And he wanted her to meet his mom. In an attempt to get to Jose's early, Cole and she had dashed out of church when the last hymn was sung to get ahead of the crowd.

She changed into jeans, a warm flannel shirt and boots. The two of them headed to the ranch a short time later.

When they reached the ranch, he directed her to park near the back door of the main house, next to the sedan his folks used on Sundays.

"I'll introduce you to my mother and you can wait here while I get changed. My place isn't far. Then we'll get a couple of horses and ride out."

"Okay." She glanced around, recognizing the barn where she'd been before. "Where is your place?"

"About a half mile beyond the barn, toward the east. You can't see the house from here."

"So you don't live with your folks?"

"No, not for some time now. And before the house was built, I slept in the bunkhouse with the other ranch hands. A man can only take so much of his mother's eagle eye."

She nodded. "Understood."

His mom had already changed into comfortable clothes and was in the living room watching a movie. She quickly turned it off when they entered.

"So nice to meet you, Jennifer. My husband speaks highly of your capabilities. You made a really good impression on him," Susan Martin greeted her.

"I'm glad. The horse is doing well last I heard."

"Doing fine. Allan's in the barn. I'll call him."

"No, don't bother. Cole asked me out to go riding, so I'll wander over there while he's changing. That way I can check the horse and see Allan all at once."

"Okay. Please plan to stay for dinner. It'll be too late for you to cook anything by the time you get back to town," Susan invited.

"Thank you, I'd like that." Jennifer smiled at Cole's mother and then looked at him. He was making a weird face at his mother, which he segued into a smile when Jennifer caught his eye.

"You okay?" she asked.

"Yeah. I'll change and meet you at the barn."

Smoky had healed with little scarring. Jennifer was pleased. He was a working horse, not a show animal, but she was glad the situation turned out well. She and Allan discussed the horse and the other stock on the ranch. Time passed swiftly and before long Cole joined them.

"We're going for a ride," he told his father.

"Cold out today."

"I know, we won't be gone long. I thought Starlight for Jennifer."

"She's a good one. You two enjoy."

Allan headed back to the house while Cole brought out a pretty buckskin mare. He handed

Jennifer the halter lead. "We'll tack up at the end of the barn. I'll get my horse."

His was a big black gelding, several inches taller than Starlight. Before long both horses were ready and raring to go.

Cole led the way toward a rise behind the house. Jennifer caught up with him and they let the horses amble along. When they reached the top, the hills rolled out before them.

"Wow, I can see forever," she said, feasting her eyes on the pretty pastoral scene. Cattle grazed in the distance, she could see a cut in the hills, and behind them mountains rose even higher.

The afternoon was delightful. They rode to see the cattle, then Cole showed her the shallow creek that wound its way through that part of the ranch.

"This is what we have to constantly monitor to make sure the cattle have water. When it freezes, we break it up, sometimes two or three times a day. But in summer, we go swimming. There's a swimming hole up stream about half a mile that's shaded by cottonwoods and the water is always cool even on the hottest day."

She smiled, wondering if she'd ever get a chance to try it out. Who knew where they'd be come summer.

It was growing dark when they returned to the barn. They took care of the horses, Jennifer doing her share grooming Starlight before turning her back into the corral where dinner waited.

By the time Jennifer drove home she was pleasantly tired from the day. And happy there'd been no emergencies.

Dinner had been fun, with Susan and Allan full of their recent trip down the Amazon. Cole urged them to talk about their plans for a trip in the spring and so they spoke of driving across Canada once they thought the weather would permit.

Susan invited Jennifer for Christmas Eve, after the midnight service at the church.

Jennifer volunteered to make the beignets, even after Susan told her how many to expect at breakfast that morning.

"Not a problem," she'd said. "In my family, there are five girls, those who are married bring their families, so my mom often makes enough for a dozen or more. I'll be ready."

But the moment she focused on was when Cole had walked her to her truck, told her goodnight and kissed her.

12

Jennifer had felt the kiss to her toes. She'd leaned in closer, savoring the sensations that swept through her. A minute later he'd pulled back slightly and she opened her eyes to gaze at his in the dim light from the stars.

"I really enjoyed today," he said softly.

"Ummm." She looked at his lips and he leaned in to gently give a quick kiss.

"I have to go," she murmured against his mouth.

"I know," he'd murmured against hers.

One more kiss and he pulled back. "Okay, that'll tide me over."

She still could feel the tingling his kisses had brought. Her face felt flushed thinking about him. She wished they could have explored those sensations a bit longer, but not there where his parents were probably wondering what was taking her so long to leave.

Jennifer had tried to see him in her rear view mirror, but it was too dark once she left the house behind. But she had no trouble picturing him in her mind. And reliving those magical kisses.

"Wow," she said as she entered her apartment and danced across the room. They might be playing make believe, but she hadn't known she'd relish a kiss like that. Or feel so alive. She wasn't at all tired after all.

She stopped suddenly.

There'd been no need for Cole to kiss her. No one had seen them. Too bad Gloria hadn't been standing nearby. Those kisses would convince anyone he was no longer caught up with his ex-girlfriend.

"It convinced me," she murmured as she took off her jacket.

Too bad it wasn't for real. A woman could go for a man who kissed like that. No wonder Gloria didn't want to let go.

Cole walked across the yard and headed home, his thoughts spinning. He hadn't planned to kiss Jennifer. But she'd looked so enticing in the semidarkness. And he had to admit more than once today he'd thought about kissing her. On their ride. Grooming the horses. Heck, even one time when she laughed at something his mother had said.

He couldn't understand how her fiancé could have proclaimed love and then turned to someone else.

Jennifer was smart, pretty, interesting and sweet. Really sweet.

He'd like to meet her sister, because he wasn't sure how anyone could top Jennifer.

Getting ready for bed he wondered when the next time he could see her would be. There was another meeting of the live nativity committee on Wednesday–probably not before then. Three days away. It seemed like a long time.

He shook his head. He was losing it.

The first part of the week flew by. Jennifer pulled into the church parking lot Wednesday night, earlier than before. Glad to see she wasn't the last as a car drove in behind her, she parked and headed for the fellowship hall. The wind blew endlessly and dropped the wind chill to below zero. She hoped it was warmer the week before Christmas for the sake of all the players and the animals. And especially for the child playing baby Jesus this year.

Teresa greeted her when she stepped inside.

"It's freezing out there," Teresa said, raising a steaming cup. "They're serving hot chocolate over there," she pointed to the side wall. "I'll save you a seat."

"Good. I need something to warm up."

Jennifer sat next to Teresa a moment later, cradling the warm cup in both hands. She'd take her jacket off in a minute, first she wanted to feel really warm.

"How do you stay outside in this weather during the live nativity? I think I'd freeze to death," Jennifer said with a smile at her friend.

"We have heaters that take the chill off, and all costumes are huge so we can wear jackets beneath them. I saw you in church Sunday, but you only had eyes for Cole Martin."

Jennifer grinned at her. "He's something else, don't you think?" Did she know how to play a role or what?

"I've always thought so. Sadly, he doesn't think the same about me."

"Oh, did you want to date him?"

Teresa laughed. "No, he's a friend. I have my sights on a cowboy on the Flying W ranch. He doesn't go to our church, but I'm working on him."

Jennifer laughed and took a sip of the hot chocolate. Warmth spread through her. She set it down and took off her jacket, draping it on the back of her chair, scanning the room to see if she saw Cole.

"He's not here yet," Teresa said teasingly.

"Oh, that obvious, huh?' Jennifer asked sitting down and picking up her cup again.

"Maybe. I see Ed, though. You two went out, right?"

"We had coffee one time."

"Not quite in Cole's league," Teresa murmured as the pharmacist ambled over toward them.

"Hi ladies," he said.

"Hi Ed," Jennifer said with a smile.

"Mind if I join you?"

"Sit right here," Teresa said patting the empty chair next to her. "And tell us how the construction plans are going."

"Same as any year," he said, taking the indicated chair. He leaned over to see Jennifer. "How was your week?"

"No emergencies to speak of." Since the only call that might have been an emergency had proved a fake.

"I saw you and the others cleaning the corral Saturday. It looks good."

Jeff walked to the front and picked up the microphone.

"Good evening."

The committee echoed the greetings.

"We'll start with prayer and then get to the updates. My goal is to keep this meeting under an hour."

When the reports began, Jennifer listened attentively. Conscious of being the new kid on the block, she wanted to pick up on everything as quickly as possible.

Jeff called on the costume designer first, and she reported on ones that could be used again and the new ones still in progress–mostly angel costumes as they had more this year than last.

One by one subcommittee chairs reported from the music director, to the construction crew to the actors. When Jeff asked about the animals, Jennifer was surprised to hear Cole report the stables were ready, animals lined up and feed arranged.

She turned around to see him in the back, standing with some other men.

He caught her eye and winked at her.

Turning around she faced forward disappointed he hadn't taken the seat to her left. Teresa had done her part to keep it empty. Two seconds later he slid into it.

"I got here in time for the report," he whispered to her. "Thought I'd be here earlier."

She nodded, keeping her eyes on Jeff.

To her surprise, Cole reached out and took her hand, lacing his cold fingers between her warmer ones. Jennifer smiled at him. Of course he'd want to demonstrate something here, the more the merrier to let Gloria know.

Teresa nudged her. Across the room Gloria stared daggers at them. Jennifer turned back to what Jeff was saying and tried to ignore the other woman. She felt sorry for her. She knew how hard–with a shock, Jennifer realized she hadn't thought of Joe once in four days. Not since before church on Sunday.

Now with Cole holding her hand, a new friend in Teresa, and being part of the live nativity, she realized she'd moved on. The hurt and disappointment had begun to fade.

She gave a quick prayer of thanks, and vowed to embrace this new stage of her life. She was actually happy.

The meeting ended within the hour Jeff had planned.

"Want to get a quick cup of coffee before I head back?" Cole asked.

"Want to come to my place? She said in return.

"Sure."

Ed and Teresa rose when they did. The pharmacist glanced once at the linked hands between Jennifer and Cole and bid them a quiet goodbye.

Cole watched him walk away. "He's a good man."

"We had coffee together last week. I hope I can count him as a friend."

"We'll see. Ready?"

"Cole!" Gloria came up to them, glaring at Jennifer.

"Hi Gloria." He didn't say another word, but his hand tightened slightly around Jennifer's.

"This meeting didn't last very long. I thought maybe we could talk."

"I have other plans. As I've told you before, Gloria, we don't really have anything to talk about."

She glanced at Jennifer and their linked hands.

"I guess not tonight. But we do need to sit down and hash things out."

"Give it up. It's not going to happen," he said gently.

She stared at him for a long moment. Then turned and walked away.

"Do you think she got the hint?" he asked as he and Jennifer headed for the door.

"Unless she needs a two by four upside the head, she got it," Jennifer said. "Rumor on the street was she tried to make you jealous, she didn't want to break up," she said.

"I was mad at first. Then I think I was disappointed at the way things turned out. But playing games doesn't make sense. What did she expect, me to rush over and punch the other guy out?"

Jennifer laughed. The wind whipped around them, and she looked at Cole. "That's funny, the part where playing games doesn't make sense. What are we doing?"

He stopped and looked at her. "I don't know. Maybe this isn't a game?"

She stared at him for a long moment. It had started as a game just days ago. What did he mean?

"The thing is, I think I'd like to see where this would go for real," he said.

"This?" She didn't know what to say. Her heart raced, her hand tightened on his. She ignored the others going to their vehicles as she stared at Cole.

"I know I asked for make believe. Stupid, now that I think about it. What about exploring a relationship for real?"

She didn't know what to say.

That was wrong, she knew exactly what she wanted to say, "Yes, I'd like that."

But would that lead to heartache again?

Her mother warned her about rebound relationships.

"I don't know. Let me think about it."

"It's freezing out here, can you think about it back at your place?"

Jennifer nodded. She hoped she could figure things out during the short distance from the church to her apartment. Right now her thoughts were in turmoil and she could only think about how she'd like him to kiss her again.

13

Cole followed Jennifer to her apartment. He hadn't known he was going to tell her how he felt. But something had changed since Sunday and he knew he wanted to get to know her better without playing games. He knew she had reluctantly agreed to help him out. It wasn't as if she rushed in to showing everyone they were a couple. Had he blown it?

If Gloria finally got the message, then he and the new vet in town didn't have to continue. But he wanted to. And when he examined the situation he realized he was taken with her, more than with anyone else he'd dated over the years.

He knew she was coming off a bad breakup. But maybe–

He wished she'd said something in the parking lot. Now he was on pins and needles wondering if she'd even let him in her apartment. Maybe she'd say if play acting wasn't needed any more, he need not stay for coffee.

Wishing he'd kept his mouth shut, he could only wait to see the outcome of his announcement.

When she parked her truck, he parked next to her. She waited at the back of her truck for him. So far so good.

"If it's this cold the nights of the live nativity, I'm staying inside. The animals will have to fend for themselves," she said as they hurried inside.

"They'll be fine. They're used to the cold, after all they're out in it all the time."

"I miss Texas on days like this," she said opening the door and stepping inside.

He picked up on that. Was it her way of saying she wouldn't be staying in Wyoming? A roundabout way to say back off.

Or even worse—forget it?

"Do you want coffee or hot chocolate?" she asked, turning to face him with a bright smile on her face.

"I think I want you," he said, reaching out to draw her into his arms and lower his face to kiss her.

From her response, doubts began to flee. She couldn't be kicking him loose if she could kiss like this.

She broke the kiss and pulled back, smiling brightly. Her eyes sparkled. Pink colored her cheeks. Cole thought she looked adorable. He didn't want the evening to end.

"So–hot chocolate or coffee?" she asked as she took off her heavy jacket as if nothing had happened between the first time she asked and the second.

Cole drew a deep breath, waiting to get his clue from her.

"Hot chocolate. Do you have marshmallows?"

"Sure do. Have a seat and I'll get some for us."

He took off his coat and followed her into the kitchen.

"I saw Hank and Tabitha again today," she said as she drew the milk from the fridge and then the cocoa mix from her cupboard.

"Bull injured for real this time?"

"No, one of Hank's cattle dogs. Got caught in barbed wire just like Smoky. You ranchers need to make sure you pick up all the tossed pieces when repairing fences."

He nodded. "It can be a problem. Try as we might, it seems as if there're always segments lying around. Although some of it's from the early days. Range land is cross fenced differently sometimes and remnants of earlier fencing that's fallen down remains. Is the dog okay?"

"He will be. But he's on the disabled list until further notice. He really cut up his paw badly. It required twenty stitches. What did you do today?"

Cole leaned against the counter watching her as the cocoa heated on the stove. "We are at full staff right now, some of the guys are taking off for Christmas. Others will hang around. Everyone wants the beignets!"

She looked at him. "How did everyone know about beignets?"

"I might have mentioned it to one or two of the men. Cowboys love donuts, didn't you know that?"

"They won't be as good as my mom's," she warned.

"But we don't have anything to compare with so we'll love them."

Cole looked forward to Christmas. He wanted to spend the day with her, even surrounded by others at the ranch. He'd pick her up after the midnight service and then take her to the ranch. His mother had already prepared the guest bedroom.

"Cole!"

He met her gaze. "What?"

"Did you hear me ask if you wanted some shortbread cookies?"

"No." He was too busy thinking about her.

"No you don't want any?"

"No, I didn't hear you I was thinking of something else. Yes, I'd love some cookies. Did you make them?"

"Yes. Actually, I love to bake. I don't cook often–not just for one. Baking, on the other hand, can be for as many people as I want. I take cookies with me sometimes if I go out on a call. And I do have regularly scheduled visits for vaccines and all. Thankfully not everything is an emergency. It's fun to surprise clients with cookies and definitely different from Dr. Hazlet."

"I'll say, I never knew him to bring cookies anywhere."

They settled on the sofa with hot chocolate and a plate of cookies.

Cole tried to keep the impatience at bay. He'd put things on the line and she still hadn't said anything. Did she want to explore a relationship? They found it easy to talk with each other. He was fascinated by every aspect of her life and wanted to know more. And she kissed like no one else he'd known.

Was she still too caught up with feelings for her ex-fiancé? Once burned like that, he could see a woman not willing to risk her heart again anytime soon.

Her heart? Was he talking heart to heart love? He glanced at the cup of hot chocolate. Yes, he wanted to explore a relationship, get to know her. But was he falling in love with her in such a short time?

Suddenly he wanted to be alone to think this through.

As soon as he finished his beverage, he rose. "I need to get home, it's still a half hour drive."

"I know. Thanks for stopping by."

He gave her a quick kiss at the door and then headed for his truck.

He sat there a moment after starting the engine. He was falling in love with Jennifer. And he hadn't a clue what she felt. Was her agreement to pretend a relationship merely to help out a new friend? Or could she fall for him? Did he need to give her time—time to get over Joe and be opened to a new relationship. Open to love?

How much time?

He wished he could ask someone, but he didn't know a soul who had had this kind of experience.

Patience was never a long suit of his, but in this case he had no choice. As long as she was silent on his question, he'd hope when she did respond that it would be what he wanted to hear.

Until then, he'd do all he could to convince her he would stay the course. That had to be the biggest hang up.

Unless she was still in love with Joe.

When Jennifer awoke on Thursday, she was surprised to see several inches of new snow. She'd heard a storm was expected, but somehow she thought the wind would blow the snow away so there wasn't so much on the ground. The snow-covered trees attested to the lack of wind.

She stepped outside. It was bitterly cold, clear and crisp. And as still as could be. The snow hushed all sounds. Taking another breath of the fresh air, she hurried back inside to get warm. There were no appointments for the day, so barring any emergencies, she could get some personal things done—like order presents online for Christmas. Or write Christmas cards to friends she probably wouldn't see this year.

Which meant she needed to let her mother know her decision about Christmas. Cole's invitation was the clincher. She'd enjoy spending the day with him and the others on the ranch. It'd be totally different from all her other Christmases. And it meant being away from home. Catherine had been in Rome last Christmas. She had enjoyed the difference in how the day was celebrated in Italy.

Jennifer sat sipping her coffee and thinking about her sister. She'd been devastated when Catherine returned home and immediately fallen for Joe. How could two people fall in love so fast. Especially Joe? He'd professed to love her. Then he switched to her sister so fast it made her head spin.

An elopement planned and carried out before anyone knew anything.

Before she could grasp the change, they were married—shining with happiness and love. While she was the one picking up the pieces, trying to cope, and understand how things had fallen apart so fast.

Christmas at the Circle M ranch would be a way to enjoy the day without feeling left out by not going home. And it gave her a strong reason to stay away from Texas which she hoped her family would accept.

Nothing would ever be the same at home. Not as long as Joe and Catherine were included.

Yet, would spending the day with Cole and his family send a wrong signal? She still didn't know how to respond to his suggestion. Dare she see how far this relationship could go? She was intrigued with the man. Looked forward to seeing him whenever she could.

Or was she interested in him solely as a rebound affair, to prove to herself she could still be attractive and interesting? Her self-worth had taken a blow with Joe's defection. Did that weigh in, too?

When in doubt, call home.

14

She dialed the familiar number, pleased when her mother answered at the first ring.

"Hi honey, how are you doing?"

"I have a snow day today," Jennifer said, explaining about the snow storm. "Unless I get a call out, I'm staying inside where it's warm."

"I hope you don't get called out, then. The roads might be treacherous if you are deliberately staying in today."

"My truck could handle the snow. But I have no appointments scheduled and my laptop's here, so I can do anything I need to do from home," she explained. "What's going on there?"

She and her mother chatted for a while about various members of the family and what each had been doing lately.

"Are you coming home for Christmas, sweetheart? You still haven't said," her mother asked.

"Actually, I've been invited to a ranch outside

of town. And I told them about our beignets and they want me to make them. Do you think I can?"

Her mother didn't answer right away. "So, no trip home for Christmas?"

"I think I'll stay here, Mom. I, um, I'm trying to fit in, meet as many people as I can and all. And I still haven't talked to the vet in the next county to work out reciprocal backups."

"Are you seeing anyone?"

"I've been on a couple of dates with a couple of different guys—one's a pharmacist like Daddy."

"And the other?"

"A cowboy, rancher I guess. He works with his father."

"And is that the ranch you'll spend Christmas at?"

Her mother was quick.

"Yeah."

"Catherine wants you to come home. We all do. We can get past this, sweetheart."

"I know, mom, but this year I think I want to see Christmas from a different perspective. I'll call that morning."

The decision was made. Talking with her mother clarified things. Plus, she really wanted to spend the day with Cole.

Maybe she also wanted to see how far this new relationship could go.

She needed to guard her heart. She didn't want to think she was falling in love just to show the world she'd moved on. Maybe the feelings she had around Cole would fade as they got to know each other better. Wasn't some of the attraction that of a good looking man paying her attention?

Her mother sighed softly. "You have to spread your wings, Jen. I'm hoping you'll want to move back to Texas at some point. More than that, however, sweet girl, I want you happy."

"I am, mom," she said. She loved her work. Was glad to be part of the live nativity, and couldn't help anticipating each time she got to spend with Cole.

"Take pictures of the live nativity for us," her mom said at the close of the conversation. "And of that cowboy you're dating!"

Jennifer laughed. "Okay, mom. I'll do just that. Give my love to Daddy."

She was still smiling when she went to get the box of Christmas cards.

Half way through her list her cell phone rang.

It was Cole.

"Hi. What's up?" she asked.

"Just checking in. We got a pile of snow last night. I'm in switching horses and about ready to ride out again. It's freezing!"

"I thought as much. I'm staying in today unless I get a call. Catching up on Christmas cards and ordering presents online. That way I can have them dropped shipped, rather than mailing them myself."

" One of the things I'm ordering is the beignet mix."

"You don't make it from scratch?"

"No, we get the basic mix from Café du Monde in New Orleans. I'll get several boxes, as I suspect y'all will like them as much as my family does on Christmas Morning."

"So we start a new tradition," he said softly.

"Maybe. I'll be sure to show your mom how to make them so if she likes them, y'all can have them for Christmases in the future."

"If you're not busy on Saturday, I thought we could ride out to Jason's and Sam's and check out the animals for the live nativity."

"I've got an appointment in the morning at 10 at the Wilson's place, but am free after that. I'd like to. What about Maizie's calf?"

"Good thought. I'll check with her folks to make sure they'll be home and we'll add her to the list of stops. Then I thought I could barbecue dinner for us."

"Barbecue? It's 20 degrees outside! I doubt it'll be much warmer on Saturday."

"It's the only cooking I do. We wouldn't eat outside, I'd just cook outside."

"If you're game, so am I. And I'm holding you to I don't have to eat outside."

"Gotta run. I'll pick you up around one."

"Good, see you then."

She was committed now on all fronts. And looking forward to Saturday.

The phone rang again. This time it was Ed Barnes.

"Hi Jennifer. How are you?"

"Doing fine, Ed, how about you?"

"Business is a bit slow today, due to the snow I'm sure. I called to see if you'd like to go out on Saturday. There's a new space movie playing in Wilcox, I thought we could have lunch and see the matinee."

"Thank you, Ed. I'm sorry I'm busy Saturday. I have an appointment in the morning for deworming and then Cole and I are checking out the animals for the live nativity. We got the corral ready last week, now I want to see those critters who will be in residence."

"Oh. How about Saturday night, then? We could have dinner and watch the last showing."

Jennifer hated to disappoint him, he'd been so nice to her since meeting her. "Sorry, I already said I'd eat with Cole."

"Oh. Maybe another time, then."

"I'm not sure, Ed. At least not for a while."

"Oh. I get it. You and Cole."

"Maybe. We'll see."

"Okay, then. I'll see you at the live nativity meeting."

"Sounds good, Ed. Thanks for thinking of me."

So maybe her feelings for Cole weren't only rebound. She didn't feel the same toward Ed as she did Cole. What did that tell her?

She should have asked her mom for advice. But she'd been afraid of what her mother would tell her.

She was a grown woman, capable of making her own decisions. And if falling in love with a cowboy was the way she chose, so be it.

Whoa—fall in love with Cole?

14

Saturday dawned cold and clear. Snow still lay on the ground, but the roads were fairly clear. Jennifer handled the deworming quickly, wanting to be home in time to change before meeting Cole.

When he arrived, Jennifer was ready and waiting in front of the apartment, to save him coming inside to get her. She hopped into his truck, greeting him–looking forward to spending the rest of the day with him.

"So where are we going first?" she asked.

"Jason's spread is closest. Then we'll hit Sam's. Maizie's folks' place is on the way to the ranch, so we'll hit there last before going home for dinner."

"Great plan."

When they reached Jason's ranch, Cole drove straight back to the barn before stopping. It looked similar to the Circle M ranch with a large corral to the side of the barn, the high double doors wide open.

"Jason?" Cole called when he got out of the truck.

"Hey." The older man came out of the barn. "Hi Doc. You here to check out my girl before the big event?"

"Hi Jason. Cole thought it a good idea for me to see the animals before they're taken to the corral in town.

"She's a sweetie. Was my kids' pony when they were young. They're both in college now, so pretty much this is her big outing for the year."

He led the way inside and through the barn to a smaller corral a short distance from the barn. A pinto pony stood near the fence, head between the rails, looking at them as they approached.

"Here's Miss Sparkle," Jason said.

"Oh, she's darling," Jennifer said. "I brought some apple slices. Is it okay if I give some to her?"

"Sure, she'll be your best friend for life. She's really gentle and was so good for my kids when they started out. Now, she's getting a bit old, but still loves people."

Jennifer handed the slices one by one to the pony who took them gently from her palm. She rubbed between her eyes. "So you and I will be seeing a lot of each other soon. You all ready for your part?"

The men discussed transportation of the animals, planning to move them all into town the next Saturday so they'd be there for the rehearsal after church on Sunday. Jennifer asked some questions about logistics and how the animals got along with each other.

"No problems in the past. That calf of Maizie's shouldn't be a problem either. It's her 4-H project and she takes it really seriously," Jason said.

They didn't stay long, heading next for Sam's ranch.

"Does Sam raise sheep? I thought this was mostly cattle country," Jennifer said as they sped down the highway.

"He has a small herd. His wife's big into using the wool for all sorts of things, weaving blankets, knitting and all. She likes the whole process from shearing to carding to the finished product. You'll see her sweaters and baby sets at the county fair next summer. She always takes home a few first place ribbons."

"Ummm. That's getting to be a lost art—from sheep to finished product. Most folks if they are into handwork like that buy yarn at a store."

"Not Natalie. She loves the entire process."

When they turned into the driveway that led to Sam's ranch, Jennifer saw several sheep grazing alongside the drive.

"You're right, it's a small herd."

Cole stopped his truck near the house and a tall woman with grey hair came out wearing a thick cable knit sweater, her arms across her chest for warmth.

"Cole, nice to see you."

"You, too, Natalie. I'd like you to meet Jennifer Carleton, our new vet."

"Hi Jennifer. Sam told me you'll be helping out at the live nativity."

"Hi Natalie, it's nice to meet you. I take it we'll be using some of your sheep."

"Yep, Betsy and Scrappy. And maybe little Amber."

"You name your sheep?" Jennifer asked a bit surprised. Usually ranchers were more pragmatic about the stock animals they raised.

"These are my babies—of course I named them. I only have a couple of dozen. Several different breeds to get different wool. Come on out to the barn. I've already gotten them ready for the live nativity."

They followed her to a large double stall in the barn. Peering over the half door, Jennifer saw three sheep munching on hay. They looked up and rose to their feet. One was quite small.

"Is that a lamb?" Jennifer asked.

Natalie nodded. "Late born, six months old now. Really sweet, so I wanted to try her out in the nativity. If she does alright, she could be included for several years. Scrappy and Betsy have been doing this for four or five years now."

"She'll take some watching, then," Cole said.

"Do we stick with the animals while they're on stage?" Jennifer asked.

"Not usually. But maybe this time—at least the first couple of nights to see how the lamb does."

"I think she'll do just fine. Sam's bringing them in next Saturday morning."

"Jason's bringing Sparkles in, too," Cole said.

"You bringing Gunner?" Natalie asked.

"Of course, that old mule wouldn't know what to do with himself if he didn't get to perform each year."

"He just likes the babying," Natalie said with a smile. She looked at Jennifer. "Have you met Gunner yet?"

"Not yet."

"We're heading out to the ranch when we leave here," Cole said.

"He's a character that's for sure. Sam told me you plan to do the morning feedings for the duration," Natalie said to Jennifer.

"Right. Easier for me, I'm right in town."

"Come on inside it's freezing out here," Natalie invited.

"We need to be heading out. Another time?" Cole said.

"Okay. See you in church."

With a wave, she hurried back inside the house.

The stop at Jamerson's was equally brief. The calf Maizie was raising was larger than the sheep, but friendly and placid.

All the different animals would make a good representation of the stable where the baby Jesus was born.

Arriving at the Circle M a short time later, Cole drove past the main house and veered right on a smaller drive. His house was built a half mile from his folks. Close enough to be there all the time, but far enough away to give each of them space.

He opened the door for Jennifer and she stepped inside.

"Oh, I like what you've done with the place," she said looking at the almost empty living room.

There was a large table and four chairs in the dining area visible beyond an archway.

"I just finished building it a year ago. I lived out of a trailer for four years while we built this. I haven't gotten around to furnishing it completely yet," he defended.

She grinned at him. "I'd say you haven't started."

"Not so. Just important things first. I have a bed and dresser and recliner in the bedroom, and a large screen TV. When I'm home that's where I hang out. And the kitchen's stocked. Come on through."

The modern kitchen was spacious and open. With large windows along the back wall, Jennifer could see rolling hills and the wide blue sky.

"This is really nice."

"And the grill's right off the back door under a lean-to so I can use it year round. Easier to throw a steak or two on it then figuring out cooking on a stove."

"Where did your mom go wrong?" she teased.

"Don't knock it until you try it." He leaned over and kissed her.

"I've been wanting to do that since I first saw you today."

She smiled and moved slowly away. Her heart was beating faster, but now was not the time to give into temptation.

"What can I do to help?" she asked.

"Maybe wash the potatoes. I'll cook them in the coals. Then we could have a salad. I bought ice cream for dessert."

"Sounds like a feast," she said.

They worked well together in preparing the meal. Jennifer even ventured outside to stand near Cole as he cooked the steaks on the grill. The lean-to was sheltered on three sides, giving plenty of ventilation but keeping them sheltered from the wind. Snow still covered most of the area around the house. The stars seemed so white against the black sky, reflecting some of their light on the snow.

"It's really pretty here," she said as she gazed over the back yard.

"I have a deck that's covered with snow right now. It's nice to sit out after dark in the warmer months and just enjoy the land."

She nodded. It sounded peaceful. A nice way to wind down after a busy day. She had a small patio off her apartment that she used during the warmer weather.

Time seemed to fly as they ate dinner and then had hot chocolate. She asked lots of questions about the live nativity and some of the other ranchers around. He told her more stories of growing up which she matched with tales of her own childhood.

"You and your sisters must have been a handful for your parents," he commented at one point.

"We did sort of egg each other on."

"You must miss them."

She nodded. "I do. But I'm making a difference here and love my practice. I hope one day folks will forget I'm the newcomer and I'll be a part of the community."

"You will. If you stay."

"Why wouldn't I stay?" she asked.

"Not saying you won't. Who knows how you'll feel down the road."

"Meaning?"

"One day you'll be over the hurt of Joe and your sister. Then maybe being closer to family will outweigh the benefits of living here."

She studied her chocolate for a moment, not knowing how to answer. Was there truth in what he said? If she got over the hurt would she rather be back in Texas?

16

"It's getting late. I'll take you home," Cole said.

She nodded and put down her cup. She wished she could reassure him she was here for good, but he raised an interesting question. Could he be right?

At church on Sunday, she and Cole sat together, this time with his parents on the right side of the church.

"Things look different from this side," she murmured to him as the service was about to begin.

"Same songs and message, though," he said back.

She and Susan spent some time in front of the church after the service discussing plans for Christmas. Jennifer explained how Cole wanted to take her to the Christmas Eve service and then they'd drive home.

"Weather permitting, Allan and I like to attend that service as well. It gets us home late, though."

"How early do I have to get up to make beignets," Jennifer asked.

Susan laughed. "Early. Those cowboys are used to getting up at dark thirty, and they always wake up hungry."

Cole joined them. "Jennifer and I are going to lunch at Jose's, do you and dad want to join us?" he said.

"No, I have a pot roast in the slow cooker. We need to get home for that. Another time. You two have fun. Jennifer was telling me about coming to the house on Christmas Eve after the last showing of the live nativity."

"Oh, I forgot," Jennifer said. "Who'll feed the animals Christmas morning? That's my job, I need to be here for that."

"We'll arrange someone else in town to zip out to make sure they're okay that one morning," Cole said. "One week from today we'll be in rehearsal and then it'll be show time."

Wednesday Cole did not attend the live nativity committee meeting. He'd called Jennifer and left a message on her phone that since his part was the same as other years and everything was lined up he didn't see the need.

She attended, glad to see Teresa again, and some of the other members she was gradually coming to know.

Jeff came over when she arrived.

"We've got a problem. Winona fell yesterday and broke her leg in two places. She has to remain off it for the foreseeable future."

"I'm sorry to hear that," Jennifer said, trying to remember who Winona was.

"She was due to play Elizabeth in that scene with Mary when they talk about the coming birth of the savior. Can you step in? It's not much. Pantomime excitement to see your cousin, happiness at the news, that kind of stuff."

"Oh, I hadn't thought to have a part. I'm helping with the animals. Shouldn't I stay with them during the program in case something happens?"

"You won't be too far away if there is anything that goes wrong, but I'd really appreciate it if you'd take that role."

She thought about it for a moment. It sounded like something she could do. "Okay."

"Great. I'll let Martha know. You'll have to see her to try on the costume over your coat to make sure it'll fit. Rehearsal's Saturday afternoon, then we go live starting Monday evening. As you know, everyone is to be here by six each evening to set up and get dressed. We open at seven to eight-thirty. If it rains or snows, we may close earlier, depending on traffic. So will you need help getting the animals here in time to get to the location of that scene?"

"Cole's in charge of transportation, I'll double check with him."

When Jennifer reached home, she called Cole.

"Hi, how was the meeting?"

"I'm going to be Elizabeth!" she blurted out. "Can I do that, I mean because of the animals and all."

"Sure. What happened to Winona?"

"She broke a leg and can't stand on it for a while. I've never been in a play before."

"At least you don't have any lines to memorize."

"True. I'm sort of excited and nervous at the same time."

"You'll do fine. Reread that scene in the Bible and you'll know as much as anyone about how to pretend to be Elizabeth."

"And the animals?"

"Before the rehearsal, we'll practice loading them up and delivering to the church. We'll identify any problems that way. Jason, Sam and Maizie will be there to help. And Sam usually hangs around the animals during the performance. It's important as the rest of us have characters to portray. We're telling the Christmas story to the whole community. And then some. Folks come over from Wilcox and some of the other nearby towns to see it, too."

"You don't have a part," she said.

"I fill in sometimes. Once I was Gabriel, another year I was a shepherd. Who knows if the need will arise this year."

"I wish my family could see it."

"I'll take a video and you can send it to them."

She laughed. "My mom will be so proud—her daughter the actress."

"Who knows, it could lead to Broadway."

Jennifer laughed again. "Right. Let's see how this goes first."

"I'm glad you agreed," Cole said.

It was another way to build stronger ties to the community. He hoped by this time next year she'd be firmly entrenched.

And never give a thought to returning to Texas.

Saturday was the day the live nativity animals were due to arrive at the town corral and Jennifer wanted to be there when they arrived. Cole said he'd be bringing Gunner around noon, and asked her to lunch. The others were due to arrive before then. They were going to discuss transportation to and from the church each day and she didn't want to miss that either. After lunch they'd have their first run at transporting the animals from the corral to the church.

A knock sounded on her door. Had Cole come early? They were supposed to meet at the corral.

To her surprise, when Jennifer opened the door, Joe stood there.

"Joe?" she asked in disbelief.

"Hi Jennifer. We need to talk."

"Talk?" She clung to the door. What in the world was he doing here? She looked beyond him; no one else in sight.

"Where's Catherine?" she asked.

"Home. She's going through morning sickness now. Not that she knows I'm here. We need to talk. *I* need to talk to you."

For a moment, Jennifer didn't know what to say. This was the man who had practically left her standing at the altar for a runaway marriage to her sister.

Strangely, she didn't experience the hurt and outrage she expected. He was a nice looking man whom she once knew well. Where were the emotions she'd thought she'd never get over? The shattering feelings that swamped her last spring?

"Come in," she said, stepping back so he could enter. She glanced at the clock. Almost time to leave to meet the others.

He took off his jacket and laid it on the back of a chair. Sitting gingerly on the edge, he waited until she sat on the sofa before speaking.

"I apologize. I'm truly sorry I hurt you. I never meant to hurt you. And you never let me apologize. You threw up walls, your family sheltered you, I couldn't get through to you to tell you. I loved you, Jennifer. I still do in a way. But I'm crazy, madly, forever in love with Catherine. Neither one of us meant for it to happen. Neither of us ever planned to hurt you like we did. I'm so sorry."

Jennifer nodded. She didn't feel much of anything as she listened to him. She glanced at the clock.

He cleared his throat and spoke again, "I know you loved me and what happened hurt you badly. I couldn't see beyond Catherine to take time to work things out. When she returned from

Italy, it was like a ton of bricks hit me. I couldn't see anyone but her. I know we should have handled things differently. But at the time, I only wanted Catherine."

If they were so in love they should have married.

She realized she never would have wanted him to marry her if he felt like that for her sister. That would have been totally wrong.

"I know it seems impossibly fast. But one look at her and I knew the difference. I knew what we had didn't compare to what I felt for her. And to continue as if nothing had changed served no one any good."

"I see," she said, not wanting to sit like a bump on a log while he apologized, but concerned she'd be late to the corral, she tried to think of what she could say to have him leave and let her get going.

"Anyway, I wanted you to know we're sincerely sorry for the way we handled things. And for hurting you so badly. I hope you'll come home for Christmas," he finished.

"I've already made other plans," she said.

"Can't you change them?"

She could. Of course she could. But she didn't want to.

She wanted to be part of the live nativity through Christmas Eve–to see all the people who came to see it, hope they'd take time to really enjoy the experience.

Then she wanted to attend the party after the last performance and go to the midnight service ringing in the birth of Jesus. Spend the night with Cole's parents and make beignets for everyone, cowboys included, on Christmas morning.

She wanted to spend the day with Cole.

She blinked and stared at Joe. Eight months ago her world ended when he walked away. Now she wanted more than anything to spend the holiday with an entirely different man, to share the celebration with a special person in her life.

Suddenly she knew exactly what Joe was talking about. She'd met Cole only a few weeks ago. And now she couldn't imagine him not a part of her life. A big part if she understood his meaning when he said they should see where this took them.

Their relationship had taken her right into love. The kind of love Joe was talking about–the kind they'd never shared.

"It's not fair to Catherine," he continued. "She's alienated from her family. Everyone's mad at us. Thanksgiving went badly and she's worried sick about Christmas. We should have handled it differently, but we didn't. All we can do now is ask your forgiveness and to heal the breach with her family."

Jennifer nodded. "I can forgive," she said slowly. "It would have been a horrible marriage if you'd married me feeling like you do about Catherine."

The entire situation could have been handled better. They could have discussed it before anything was done. To elope had stunned the entire family–Jennifer the most.

Time had given some perspective. Time and distance.

And Cole.

"Joe, thank you for coming," she said gently, a sense of urgency growing. She wanted to get to the corral, she wanted to be included in the discussion and in planning. Mostly she wanted to see Cole again. To see if she really had fallen in love that was blindingly strong, sure, and everlasting. Had Joe's decision all those months ago propelled her into something even better?

"Your family misses you, Jennifer. I miss you. Not in the way we once were, but we were also friends. I hate knowing you hate me."

"I don't hate anyone, Joe. I was hurt. And disappointed and totally upset. But I've found a new place for me. I won't make it home this year, but maybe next year. Or for Easter or just for a weekend sometime. I still have to arrange for another vet to cover my patients if something happens while I'm gone. I really need to do that. I keep talking about it. Never mind. I understand the situation better and while I hated what happened, I don't hate you. Or Catherine. The heart knows what it knows and obviously it chose the best for you."

Leaving the best for me to find myself. Which I have.

She took a breath. She'd changed. Her feelings had changed. All because of Cole.

"I'll be back for a visit one day," she said again.

"But not Christmas?"

"Not this year." She looked at the clock again. "I can't stay. I'm expected somewhere about now and need to go. Maybe later?"

"So we're okay?"

"Better than okay, Joe. We're good." She rose, wanting to push him out the door, but politeness ruled. "How long are you staying?" she asked as he put on his coat.

"I'm not. I'm going right back. I don't want to leave Catherine alone for long."

"When's the baby due?' she asked. Hurry, hurry she silently urged.

"We just found out before Thanksgiving, still months away, due in June."

"Give Catherine a hug from me," she said at the door. Then reached out to give him a hug. At one time they'd been close. And before that they'd been friends. Time had changed everything, but he was still a good man trying to do right by decisions made. "Thank you for coming. I am really glad to hear how it happened." To get closure.

And to know things had definitely changed for her!

As soon as his car left, she threw on her heavy jacket and headed out to meet the others at the corral. And to see Cole. She couldn't wait to see Cole!

17

Jennifer was the last to arrive. Sam had a large truck parked near the opening to the corral, unloading his sheep. As she got out of her truck, she saw Jason and Cole holding on to the halters of a pony and donkey. Maisie's dad pulled in right next to her with a bawling calf in the back of the small trailer.

She smiled and turned to offer help with getting the calf into the corral.

Once accomplished, she headed over to Cole and Jason.

"Hi," she said with a bright smile. She reached out to pet the donkey. "This is Gunner, I take it."

"Right," Cole said nodding.

She greeted Jason and the pony, then looked back at Cole. She wished they could be alone to talk.

When Sam hollered for help, Maizie and Jason went to help.

"You look especially happy today," Cole said, taking the pony's halter lead when Jason went to help Sam. Once the animals were safely in the corral they'd let them mingle.

"Joe came to see me," she said.

"Your Joe?" He asked, startled.

She nodded. "We need to talk."

"Why did he come?" Cole asked.

"To talk about Christmas."

"Hi Jennifer, Cole," Maizie came up to them. "So what's the next step, loading them all up and getting them to the church?"

"After lunch," Cole said. "We'll give them time to mingle and get used to one another. You didn't feed the calf yet, did you?"

"No. Can't you hear him bawling his head off. He's hungry."

"So we feed them now so they'll associate this place with food and be easier to handle each day," Cole said.

He wasn't sure he wanted to hear what Jennifer had to say. She looked as happy as he'd ever seen her.

Had Joe changed his mind? What a mess that would be.

Yet what else could account for her happiness?

"Jeff called this morning, he wanted us at the church by one," Sam said ambling over now that all the animals were safe in the corral.

"How do you want to work this?" Jason asked joining the group.

"Let's get a quick lunch, then see if we can load everyone on Sam's trailer, it's the largest. And I need to check that the barn area is secure at the church," Cole said, stepping away from Jennifer, focusing on the task at hand.

Time enough later to find out what Joe's visit meant.

In fact, he'd like to put it off indefinitely. Hold on to the hope he had just a little longer.

Cole did his best to keep away from Jennifer as the day progressed. Jason went for takeout at the diner and they all ate standing near the corral. Once done, Cole said he needed to check the barn and headed for church, leaving the others to round up the animals and bring them over.

By the time the animals arrived and were settled, the pony and donkey tethered, the others in the small enclosure, it was time for Maizie and Jennifer to get their costumes and assume their places in the vignettes.

Twice Jennifer had tried to talk to him, but he'd brushed her off. As if delaying the inevitable would change anything.

If he could make it through the live nativity, he'd count that as good.

His parents would be disappointed if she didn't come for Christmas. But if what he suspected was true, Jennifer wouldn't be around for long.

What else could account for the bubbling happiness that shone from her?

Jennifer was totally frustrated. She donned the robe and covering for her part as Elizabeth. Teresa was there, assisting Martha with all the costumes.

"I'm glad you could take this role," she said as she helped Jennifer get the robes over her heavy jacket. "Winona has done it for years and I know she's missing being part of the performances, but you'll do great."

"This of course makes me look like some kind of a whale with all the stuff beneath it," Jennifer complained lightly.

Teresa smiled. "Well, Elizabeth was pregnant, so even more fitting that you look large with child."

"She wasn't that far along as I remember. I'm a bit nervous."

"Hey, you'll do great. Just remember every time a new car arrives to start all over again. Maizie's playing Mary in that scene. You and she will have loads to talk about. She's in 4-H with the other kids and they are all crazy about animals."

"I know. She has her calf in with the animals at the barn. So we can talk?" Jennifer asked.

Teresa laughed. "Yes, of course. Just play your part, but you two can talk, just not loudly. The cars have the recording playing, so as long as you aren't too loud, no one will hear you."

"How come you don't have a starring role?" Jennifer asked as the last of her scarf was fastened.

"I'm a back up angel. As if we don't already have a gazillion. Almost every one of the youth is either a shepherd or angel. The Bible speaks of multitudes, which is what we have."

"Fun for the kids," Jennifer said.

The rehearsal went well, according to Jeff. He and the choir director had driven around several times, stopping to tweak one scene or another, or compliment the actors.

Jennifer enjoyed getting to know Maizie better and they soon had a lively, though quiet, discussion going about horses.

By the time she returned the costume to Martha and Teresa, the animals had been loaded and returned to the corral.

She drove over there. Jason and Maizie were still there but the others were gone.

"Did Cole leave?" she asked.

"He had some things to see to, so he took off as soon as we got the animals to the church," Jason said. "You're okay to handle the feeding tomorrow?"

"Yes. I'll feed them before church. I'm all set."

"Good. See you tomorrow then."

Jennifer drove home, her earlier excitement fading. Had she totally misunderstood what Cole had said a few days ago? She recalled his words. It sounded like he wanted them to make their pretense real. Yet today was totally out of line with that. If anything he seemed to avoid being around her.

She called him after dinner. But there was no answer.

Tomorrow for sure she'd ask him if everything was okay. And tell him about Joe's visit.

Sunday was cold and windy. Jennifer worried about the wind during the coming week. It was cold enough yesterday afternoon in the space she and Maizie were in, but in the wind after dark, it could really be uncomfortable.

No sense worrying about it. What would be would be.

To her surprise, she didn't see Cole or his parents at church. Had something happened?

She tried calling again and ended up leaving a message for him to call her.

Monday night was the first performance of the live nativity. Spirits were high. The weather cooperated and there was no wind and a bit of a warming trend, if rising to just below freezing could be called warming.

Jennifer had a great time. The minutes flew by. Afterward there was hot chocolate for all the participants when they turned in their costumes.

Each night had a steady stream of cars from opening to close to eight thirty. Jennifer had no idea so many people lived nearby.

"Some come every night," Maizie said wisely. "My folks do for one. My brother's a shepherd and they love taking videos of us to show the rest of the family. Of course my grandparents and aunts and uncles drive through themselves, so they've seen it live."

"I need someone to tape me," Jennifer said. "I'd love for my folks to see it. In fact, I wish the entire production was taped so they could get a feel for it."

"Jeff does that. He'll give you a copy if you ask. Sometimes the local TV station will run it on Christmas day."

Wednesday night Jennifer was surprised to see Cole returning a costume. She wondered if she should go over to speak to him. Deciding the ball was in his court, she turned away and got out of her costume. She'd have some hot chocolate and go home. If he didn't want to talk to her–

"Hey," Cole said standing next to her.

She looked up. "Hi. Did you play a role tonight?"

"Gabriel again. Phil had to go out of town unexpectedly. So I'm the archangel for a few nights."

She nodded, handing her costume to Teresa.

"Staying for hot chocolate?" Cole asked.

Jennifer nodded.

"We need to talk, I believe," he said.

She glanced at him. "I called a couple of times."

"I know. This is my return. I thought we should meet in person, not discuss anything over the phone. Get your chocolate and we can go to one of the Sunday School rooms for privacy."

18

They took their hot chocolate into one of the empty rooms down the hall from the fellowship hall. Cole closed the door behind them.

"So, Joe came to visit," he said. "And you were happy to see him?"

She took a sip of the hot beverage, stalling, not sure what to say. It had been so clear on Saturday, but subsequent events had her doubting herself and Cole.

"At first I was surprised. I didn't know he was coming."

"And why did he come?"

She thought about it a moment. "For forgiveness mostly, I think. And to ask me to come home for Christmas."

"Are you going?" he asked.

She shook her head. "No. I already have plans. Right?"

"If you want to go home, go."

"Actually I want to finish the run of the live nativity, attend the midnight service and then make beignets for you and your family."

He sipped his hot chocolate, studying her over the rim of the cup.

"And then?"

"Then what?"

"Are you returning to Texas?"

"At some point, I'm sure to go home to see my family. Joe and Catherine's baby is due in June. I'll be an auntie again and will want to see the baby. I definitely need to get backup by then."

"So Joe didn't come to see if you two could get back together?" he asked, setting his cup on the nearby table.

Jennifer swallowed the last of her hot chocolate and put her cup beside his. "No and if he had I would have said no."

"What?"

She faced him "It was weird at first seeing him, but the most astonishing part of the entire visit was my feelings. There wasn't any crushing hurt, no anger, no emotions pretty much at all. I was more worried about getting to the corral to meet you—I mean the group."

"What did he say?"

"He and Catherine fell in love when she returned from Italy and neither meant for it to happen. The thing is, if he'd gone through with marrying me, it would have been horrible—since he loves her. From the way he talked, they have more love than he and I ever would have."

"Still, you must wish things had ended differently."

She stepped closer and touched his jacket. "Actually I think I'm exactly where I'm supposed to be. And with someone special who—"

He leaned over and kissed her. Taking her into his arms, he deepened the kiss.

When they drew back, both were breathing hard.

"You were saying?" he asked resting his forehead against hers.

"I realized within minutes of his showing up that my feelings for Joe were nothing like what I feel for—"

"For?"

She gazed into his eyes. "For you?"

"Is that a question?"

"Maybe. Maybe I'd like to know a bit more about that comment you made a few days ago, about seeing where this would lead us."

He kissed her again.

"It meant I love you and didn't want to pretend we were a couple. I wanted it to be for real. I hoped given time you'd come to feel something for me."

"I do. Seeing Joe again made it all clear. He's a nice man. He's happy with Catherine. We might have had a quiet happy marriage, but the sparks I feel around you were missing. And I didn't know there were sparks until you."

He laughed and swung her around. "I'll show you sparks. If you'll let me. I'm a rancher with deep roots in Wyoming. I'm never moving to Texas. But I'd cherish you all my life if you stay."

She gazed into his eyes, her face beaming with happiness. "I have no plans to move anywhere."

Then her expression grew serious.

"But much as I think I love you, is it all an illusion? Is it just a rebound feeling like my mother said I'd find?"

"What do you mean?"

"I loved Joe and was going to marry him. I wasn't the one who called it off. Today, I felt nothing like that love for him that I once felt. You were crowding my mind, You were the one I wanted to see. But what if this isn't any more lasting than my feelings for Joe? What if—"

"And what if it's not. What if this time love will last forever?"

"I do love you. I know I do."

"Maybe you need a little time to convince yourself," he said. "I'm not in any great rush. I'm going to be here next to you as long as you let me. And if you become convinced at some point, then we'll discuss the next step."

"Like?"

"Like wait and see. Mostly I want to love you and make a life with you. You're right, however, we both need to be sure. So, let's see how far this relationship will take us."

"Deal, cowboy," she said, hugging him close and lifting her face for his kiss.

One Year Later

"I have butterflies in my stomach and I think I'm going to faint," Jennifer said, staring at herself in the full length mirror. The shimmering bridal gown looked amazing. Her hair was up and the small hat with veil gave her a glow that every bride should have.

"Why you wanted to have the wedding on Christmas Eve is beyond me," her mother said, shifting the veil slightly, then letting it fall back in place.

"It's the night Cole proposed—sort of."

"And once the reception is over, you're heading back outside for the live nativity. I never heard of such a thing."

Jennifer laughed, turning to hug her mother. "It's our thing."

"Hmmph. Most newly married couples take off for their honeymoon."

"We're going the day after Christmas. This suits us, Mom."

"I'm sure it does. You look radiant. I'm happy for you, sweetie."

"I'm so happy. More than I ever thought I could be."

Her mother nodded.

"More than I was with Joe," Jennifer said slowly. "I invited Catherine and Joe, but they didn't come."

"I know. I think there's some lingering guilt and embarrassment with them. Give them time, they'll come around. And here we are—another Christmas without you at home."

Jennifer laughed again. "I know, but Mom, everyone else is here, too, so it'll be a great Christmas. And you don't have to do all the cooking. Susan is delighted to have us all at the ranch. She loves to cook."

Her dad knocked and then opened the door. "Ready, sweetheart?"

"I am," Jennifer said, turning to smile at him.

And she was. The last year had flown by. She and Cole had become inseparable. They found they had many interests in common and loved the same activities like riding, hiking or sitting around on a cold night and watching old black and white movies. Their love had grown and deepened as the months went by. She was glad he'd been proven right—this love was nothing like what she'd known before.

As she walked down the aisle she only had eyes for Cole, standing at the altar waiting for her. Her heart filled with joy and love. All doubts fled. She was going to marry the man she loved.

His smile was contagious. She smiled back. Soon they'd become husband and wife; complete their part in the live nativity; celebrate Christmas with both families and then begin their lives together.

When Cole reached out to take her hand, he squeezed gently and leaned a bit closer.

"This is looking to be the best Christmas ever."

"A very special Christmas," she agreed, turning to face the minister, knowing it was just the first of many. Their future was bright with love, hope and promise.

Did you enjoy this story?
If so you may enjoy **A Soldier's Christmas**

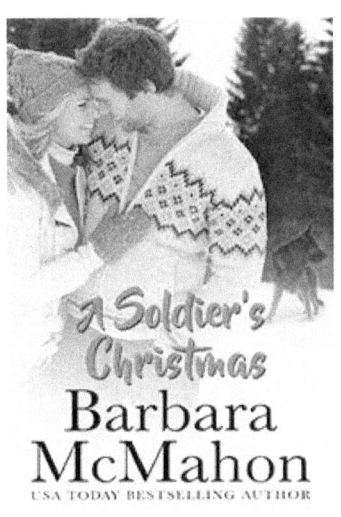

If you enjoyed **The Cowboy's Special
Christmas,** please consider leaving a review.

For a complete list of Barbara's books, please visit
www.barbaramcmahon.com.